RUFUS AT THE DOOR

& OTHER STORIES

BY JON HASSLER

Staggerford
Simon's Night
The Love Hunter
A Green Journey
Grand Opening
North of Hope
Dear James
Rookery Blues
The Dean's List
My Staggerford Journal
Keepsakes & Other Stories

FOR YOUNG READERS

Four Miles to Pinecone
Jemmy

FORTHCOMING

Days Like Smoke: Recollections of a Happy Boyhood
On Goodness: Sketches from a Novelist's Life
Stories Teachers Tell

RUFUS AT THE DOOR

& OTHER STORIES

JON HASSLER

WOOD ENGRAVINGS BY
GAYLORD SCHANILEC

AFTON HISTORICAL SOCIETY PRESS
AFTON, MINNESOTA

Library of Congress Cataloging-in-Publication Data

Hassler, Jon.
        Rufus at the Door and other stories / Jon Hassler; wood engrav-
ings by Gaylord Schanilec.
        p.   cm.
    Contents: Rufus at the Door -- Anniversary -- Winning Sarah
Spooner -- The life and death of Delano Klein -- Dodger's return --
Agatha McGee and the St. Isidore Seven -- Nancy Clancy's nephew.
    ISBN 1-890434-28-0 (hc) -- 1-890434-29-9 (pb)
    I. Minnesota -- Social life and customs -- Fiction. I. Title: Rufus at
the door and other stories. II. Title.

PS3558.A726 R84   2000
813'.54--dc21   00-024318
                                                                      CIP

Printed in Canada.

"Rufus at the Door" first appeared in *Stiller's Pond* (New Rivers Press), "Anniversary" in *Redbook*,
"Dodger's Return" in *Twin Cities* magazine, "Nancy Clancy's Nephew" in *North American Review*,
"Winning Sarah Spooner" in *Image*, and Agatha McGee's holiday letter in the *St. Paul Pioneer Press*.

The Afton Historical Society Press is a non-profit organization that takes
pride and pleasure in publishing exceptional books on regional subjects.

W. Duncan MacMillan   Patricia Condon Johnston
president   publisher

Afton Historical Society Press
P.O. Box 100
Afton, MN 55001
800-436-8443
e-mail: aftonpress@aftonpress.com
www.aftonpress.com

For George Thibault

PUBLISHER'S NOTE

ONCE UPON A TIME, before Atheneum in New York took a chance on an unknown author and published *Staggerford* (1977), Jon Hassler wrote twenty-some short stories. He recalls exactly the day he began writing. It was September 10, 1970. He was thirty-seven years old and a teacher at Brainerd Community College. "I finished teaching my nine o'clock freshman English class and went to the library. I took out a notebook and pen, and began a story. I badly needed to write, but I had never taken a writing course, so I had a lot to learn."

A few of Jon's stories eventually made it into print, but he received 85 rejection slips. Jon would later incorporate some of these stories into his novels, and he stored them away "in an old wooden filing cabinet I bought for $25 at a now-defunct department store in Brainerd." That cabinet accompanied Jon to Collegeville, where he taught Minnesota Authors and Creative Writing for seventeen years at St. John's University, and to his current home in Minneapolis, where he lives with his wife, Gretchen.

Jon went on to become a favorite American novelist, and in 1998 I asked him if he would write our annual Afton Historical Society Press holiday book. Our vision for this series was that it would comprise holiday memoirs by significant Minnesota writers. Jon was only the second writer I approached. The year before, we had published Bill Holm's *Faces of Christmas Past*, a memoir—as I had asked for—about Christmases in the Icelandic community of Minneota, Minnesota.

Yes, Jon said. He would be glad to write a holiday memoir, and that was that, or so I thought. Then a few weeks before I expected his manuscript, Jon called to say that it had turned into a short story. Was that OK? I didn't have to think about this. Yes, definitely, it was. We would simply enlarge upon our original idea for our holiday series to include short fiction. We would have been out of our minds to turn down Jon's first short story in twenty years.

Like so much of Jon's work, his holiday book, *Underground Christmas*, is largely autobiographical and concerns his son David (Bob in the book) and a Christmas the two of them spent together one year. Jon (Jay in the book) is recovering from a painful divorce and Bob is living in a treatment center. Jay buys their Christmas dinner at a fast-food diner in this poignant tale, which is truly a masterpiece. *Underground Christmas* was published to rave reviews and became our best-selling book ever. Then Jon told me about his earlier stories, the ones he had in the wooden filing cabinet and asked me if I wanted to read them.

Last year (1999), Afton published seven of these twenty-some-year-old stories in *KEEPSAKES & Other Stories*, again to overwhelming response. Fans lined up out the doors at many of the book signings we scheduled throughout Minnesota. We had planned to print five thousand copies of the hardcover edition of *KEEPSAKES*, but at the last minute, with prepublication orders pouring in, we upped our print run to seven thousand. Even so, demand for Jon's stories so outstripped our expectations that we placed a print order for ten thousand softcover copies of *KEEPSAKES* before Christmas.

We also decided to give readers more of a good

thing. *RUFUS AT THE DOOR* is our second book of short stories from Jon's filing cabinet and a companion volume to *KEEPSAKES*. The title story is the heart-wrenching tale of a good-natured, slow-witted man of about thirty-five who made his first appearance in Jon's novel *Grand Opening*. "That book only covered one year, and I wanted to know more about Rufus," Jon said, "so I extended his story into the future."

Jon had actually known Rufus, during the eight years he and his family lived in Plainview, Minnesota, beginning when Jon was ten. Rufus's real name was Clarence Kronebush, and his mother routinely left him at the small Red Owl grocery store Jon's parents owned and operated while she went about her shopping. The Sunday picnic incident Jon writes about—when Rufus is taunted by his young cousins and flies into a rage and chases after them with a bread knife—not only really happened, it rocked Plainview. Rufus (Clarence) would have to be put away—taken to the asylum for the feeble-minded in Faribault, townspeople insisted—but his protective mother refused to hear of it. If anybody was coming to take Rufus away, it would be over her dead body.

That same year in Plainview, Jon's teacher took his class on a field trip to the very State Asylum for the Feeble-Minded in Faribault where people wanted to institutionalize Clarence. Leading Jon and the others from ward to ward, he had pointed out "the morons and idiots and imbeciles," while describing the differences between the various classifications. "Doesn't that sound medieval?" Jon says today.

Jon had no idea when writing "Rufus at the Door"

what had actually happened to Clarence. He was only certain that if Clarence had outlived his mother, he must have known unhappiness. Fortunately for Clarence, fate was kinder to him than Jon's fiction. On a recent visit to Plainview, Jon inquired about Clarence and his mother and learned that by the time Mrs. Kronebush died, the town had a rest home. And it was there, not in an asylum, that Clarence passed his last days quite peacefully, perhaps even happily.

Many but not all of the characters in Jon's fiction are based on people or composites of people he has known. He created those in "Anniversary," "Winning Sarah Spooner," and "The Life and Death of Delano Klein" out of thin air. "Anniversary" is the sad tale of a teacher who let life pass him by. Jon had read a story in a similar vein by John Cheever entitled "The Swimmer" and wanted to write one like it. He read Cheever over and over when he was teaching himself to write and admires him still: "I really like his sentences and his inventive ways of describing people."

About "Winning Sarah Spooner," Jon says: "I can't account for the origins of either Sarah or Emmett. I was interested in gardening at the time, and I remember using a house and a neighborhood I had lived in several years earlier in Fosston—so the location, particularly the garden in the back yard, was all I had to go on. That and Thomas Hardy's novels which I was reading at the time. Of course my characters read mostly what I read." Sarah, in the story, is a widow whose husband Byron had been a bird lover, and she feeds a variety of birds at the carousel-like birdfeeder he made and erected in their back yard. Not surprisingly, Jon Hassler is also partial to birds: "Birds are one of our great gifts in life. They sing for us and lift our spirits with their buoyancy in the air."

Where Delano Klein in "The Life and Death of . . ." came from is a mystery even to Jon. "I was in kind of a perverse mood when I wrote that story. A reviewer of my work has said that I have a rare talent for making good people interesting, which I guess is true, but I'm also fascinated by bad people as well. I don't pretend to know why Delano Klein is such a disappointment to everybody he knows. He's like Iago in *Othello*; he's just plain evil and nobody knows how he got that way."

Agatha McGee, on the other hand, is Jon's most enduring and popular character. "Agatha McGee and the St. Isidore Seven" was written for *McCalls* magazine, which had purchased two of his earlier Agatha stories but turned this one down. It was originally titled "The Striking Profile of Agatha McGee" and concerns a school strike.

Jon had experienced a three-week teachers' strike at Brainerd Community College in 1979: "We had a brand new campus outside of town, which meant we had to picket among the pine trees, where hardly anyone saw us. I later made this strike the centerpiece of *Rookery Blues*."

Agatha, Jon says, is part his mother, part his mother's maiden aunt Elizabeth "who taught school in the East and used to come visit us in the summertime," and part Hassler himself. When Jon had difficulty adjusting to the changes in the Catholic Church brought on by Vatican II, for instance, so did Agatha:

"I couldn't reconcile myself to the changes. Then along came Agatha and I poured all that resentment into

Agatha. In *Staggerford* she's still carrying her missal to Mass, reading the Latin. From that point on I was fine. As long as I knew she was carrying on in the old way, I didn't have to anymore."

Dodger, in "Dodger's Return," is another person from Jon's past—one who has nagged at him since childhood, in fact. Dodger was actually a friendless boy named Satch who lived in Plainview where he and Jon were playmates for about three days. He was known as a petty thief, and most parents had warned their youngsters away from him. "So the minute I turned up in town he was instantly my pal, coveting my toys, my love," Jon remembers. "As a newcomer, I was happy enough to have him as a friend, but as soon as I began to be taken up by a better class of friends I dumped him."

Satch or "Dodger" stayed on Jon's mind, and "he developed into a much more important character in fiction than he was in my life," Jon says. In "The Return of . . .", Dodger remains a shady character, even as an adult, but Jon's conscience continued to gnaw at him for the shabby way he had treated Satch. When Jon reinvented Dodger for his book *Grand Opening*, Dodger became a good-hearted thief who is taken in by Brendan's family and dies in a fire in their small grocery store.

George Post in "Nancy Clancy's Nephew" is modeled after Jon's maternal grandfather, Frank Callinan, a man whom he has called "the one genuine character" in his ancestry, "a man needing no adornment when transferred to the novel he starred in [*Grand Opening*]." Frank Callinan had been a conductor on the Milwaukee Road until officials discovered that he had been letting his friends ride free of charge between Austin and Minneapolis and he was fired on the spot. Nancy Clancy is based on an Irish maiden aunt, Nellie Melvin, who lived among her antiques in St. Paul to a very great age.

Six years ago, Jon Hassler was diagnosed with Parkinson's disease. In her holiday letter to Jon's friends in 1999, Agatha McGee wrote that the novelist's dreadful companion, Dr. Parkinson, "has begun to behave in cruel and irritating ways." This being the finest holiday letter I have ever read, I asked Jon if we might include it in *RUFUS*, following his stories. *See page 124.*

Jon's ambition now is to get everything he's written between covers, and we at the Afton Press are taking this task seriously to heart. *RUFUS AT THE DOOR* brings to fifteen the number of stories we have published by Minnesota's most beloved novelist. I'm very glad that Jon Hassler began writing that fateful day in September, of course. I'm glad he saved his stories. And I'm grateful beyond words that he has allowed us to publish them.

Patricia Condon Johnston

CONTENTS

RUFUS AT THE DOOR   21

ANNIVERSARY   34

WINNING SARAH SPOONER   42

THE LIFE AND DEATH OF DELANO KLEIN   58

DODGER'S RETURN   69

AGATHA MCGEE AND THE ST. ISIDORE SEVEN   91

NANCY CLANCY'S NEPHEW   107

POSTSCRIPT: A LETTER FROM AGATHA MCGEE   124

RUFUS AT THE DOOR

EACH YEAR the ninth and eleventh grades of Plum High School were loaded on a bus and driven to Rochester for a tour of what was then called the insane asylum. The boys' health teacher, Mr. Lance, and the girls', Miss Sylvestri, led us single file through a series of gloomy wards and hallways where we were smiled at, lunged at, and jeered by all manner of the mentally deficient. I recall much more about my ninth grade trip than I do about my eleventh. I recall, for example, how the faces of the retarded absorbed the elderly Mr. Lance, how he gazed at them the way we freshmen did, as though he were seeing them for the first time, and yet how he displayed none of our pity or shock or revulsion; his gaze, like a good many of those it met, was intense but neutral. I remember the middle-aged Miss Sylvestri bouncing along

at the head of our column and—as though reading labels at the zoo—calling out the categories: "These are morons, class, and over there you have the imbeciles. In the next room they're all insane." I remember my relief when the tour ended, for the place had given me a severe stom-achache. As we boarded the bus, Miss Sylvestri turned back for a last look and waved cheerily at a balloonlike face peering out the window of the broad front door and said, "That's a waterhead, class, and now we'll go down-town for lunch."

Mr. Lance drove the bus and Miss Sylvestri stood at his shoulder and delivered an unnecessary lecture about how lucky we were to have been spared from craziness and retardation. She wore a long coat of glistening black fur, and the shape of her tall hat fit the definition, in our geometry text, of a truncated cone. She asked if any of us realized that we had a moron living in Plum.

Pearl Peterson's hand shot up. Pearl was the ninth grade's foremost sycophant. "Henry Ahman," she said. "Henry Ahman is a moron."

"No, I'm sorry, Pearl. Henry Ahman is an epileptic, there's no comparison. Come now, class, I'm asking for a moron."

I knew the right answer, but I kept my mouth shut for fear of losing face with my friends. This was the year a lot of us boys were passing through our anti-achievement phase. We had taken an oath never to raise our hands.

"Please, Miss Sylvestri," said Pearl, "would you tell us again what a moron is?"

Swaying with the traffic, Miss Sylvestri said that morons were a little smarter than idiots and a lot smarter than imbeciles. She said that morons could do things like run errands for their mothers while idiots and imbeciles couldn't leave the house. Sometimes imbeciles couldn't even get out of bed.

The impassive Mr. Lance found his way downtown and parked in front of the Green Parrot Cafe. He looked into the mirror that showed him his whole load, even those of us way in the back, and he said, "Chow time." But Miss Sylvestri begged to differ. She said nobody was having lunch until somebody came up with a moron.

My friends and I groaned anonymously.

Pearl suggested the Clifford girl.

"No, I'm sorry, the Clifford girl is an out-and-out imbecile."

Somebody else, a junior, said, "Gilly Stone."

"No, Gilly Stone's problem is polio."

Finally out of hunger—the jolting bus had settled my stomach—I shouted, "Rufus Alexander."

"That's correct—Rufus Alexander. He's very low on the scale but he's still higher than an idiot. He's what you call a low-grade moron."

We were permitted to eat.

At the west edge of Plum, Rufus Alexander lived with his mother in a little house near the stockyards. Rufus was about thirty-five and his mother was very old, yet his hair was turning gray at the same rate as hers. On Saturday afternoons they walked together to the center of the village to shop—the tall, bony-faced Mrs. Alexander striding along with her shoulders hunched and her skirts flowing around her shoetops; her tall, grinning son stepping along at her side, his back so straight that he seemed about to tip over backwards. Though he walked fast to keep pace, there was in each of his footsteps an almost imperceptible hesitation, a tentativeness that lent a jerky aspect to his progress down the street and reminded me of old films of the Keystone Kops. Whenever he came to a stop, he always clasped his hands behind his back and stood as though at attention; from a distance, in his long gray coat and white scarf, he might have been mistaken for a diplomat or a funeral director. At home Rufus sat in a deep chair by the front window and listened all day to the radio. Passing the house on my bike, I used to see him there, looking out and grinning. Mrs. Alexander had raised three older sons, but it was Rufus she loved best. He was hard of hearing and mute, though on rare occasions he made guttural noises which his mother took to be words.

In order to go about her Saturday shopping unencumbered by Rufus, who couldn't turn a corner without being steered, Mrs. Alexander would deposit him either in the pool hall or in my father's grocery store. She would look in at the pool hall first, because there Rufus could sit on one of the chairs around the card table, but if she saw that her card-playing son—her oldest son, Lester—hadn't come to town, she would lead Rufus down the street to our store and place him in my father's care.

Not that he needed care. He was content to stand at the full-length window of the front door, looking out. For as long as two hours he would remain there as though enchanted, his hands clasped behind him, his eyes directed at a point slightly above the passing people, his face locked in its customary grin. When someone entered or left the store—Rufus would shuffle backward and allow himself to be pressed for a moment between the plate glass in front of him and the glassine doors of the cookie display behind him, and then as the door went shut he would shuffle forward, keeping his nose about six inches from the glass.

Although our customers were greeted week after week by this moronic face, and although he obscured the cookie display, I don't think Rufus had an adverse effect on our business. Everybody was used to him. In a village as small as Plum the ordinary population didn't outnumber the odd by enough to make the latter seem all that rare. We became, as villagers, so accustomed to each other's presence, so familiar with each other's peculiarities, that even the most eccentric among us—Henry Ahman, who had fits in public; the Clifford girl, who was an out-and-out imbecile—were considered institutions rather than curiosities. I noticed that most of our customers ignored Rufus as they came through the door, while a few, like me, gave him a fleeting smile in return for his incessant grin.

He had an odd face. His round, prominent cheekbones were rosy, healthy-looking, but his eyes were skeletal—deep-set eyes under brows like ledges, blue eyes perfectly round and (I thought at first) perfectly empty. I never saw him—except once—that he wasn't grinning. Though I told myself that this was an unconscious grin, that he probably grinned all night in his sleep, I couldn't help responding to it. Returning time and again to the store after carrying out groceries, I smiled. As an exercise in will power, I would sometimes try to control this reflex. Facing Rufus as I opened the door, I would tell myself that his grin was not a sign of good will but an accident of nature, and I would attempt a neutral stare, like Mr. Lance's, but it was no use. (I could never resist smiling at clowns either, even though I knew their joy was paint.) I asked my father one time if he thought Rufus ever had anything on his mind, if he understood what he was staring at—or staring slightly above. My father said he wondered the same thing himself and had concluded that Rufus was only two-dimensional; there was no depth to him at all. And this, for a time, I believed.

Then one Monday morning—it was around the time of my first trip to the insane asylum—word spread through the town that Rufus had another dimension after all. It was said that during a Sunday picnic in Lester Alexander's farmyard, Rufus had flown into a rage. The picnic was attended by scads of Alexanders from far and near, and three or four of his little cousins began to taunt Rufus. They made up a song about his ignorance and sang it to him again and again. He rolled his great round eyes, it was said, and he made a mysterious noise like a groan or a belch (it was not reported whether he lost his grin) and he set out after the cousins, brandishing the long knife his mother had brought along for slicing open her home-made biscuits. Hearing about it, I couldn't believe that anyone had actually been in danger. I pictured Rufus tipping backward as he ran, too slow to catch his quick little cousins; I pictured the knife—a bread slicer, dull at the tip; I pictured the many Alexander men—strapping farmers all—who could easily have restrained him. But on the other hand, I could also imagine the alarm. I had attended a few of these farmyard picnics, invited by friends, and I imagined how it must have looked to a bystander: the afternoon hazy and hot; dozens of relatives deployed across the sloping, shady lawn; the children shirtless under their bib overalls; the women at the outdoor table, uncovering their tepid hot-dishes and their runny gelatins; the men smoking under the trees; then suddenly this heightened racket among the children and everyone turning and see-ing, to their terror, the youngsters scattering and shrieking (half in fright, half in glee) and Rufus hopping jerkily over the grass, the bread-knife in his hand, the blade glinting in the sun as he thrust it stiffly ahead of him, stabbing the air. As it was told the next day, Rufus's wild mood quickly passed and a half hour later he and the smaller children, full of food, lay down together for a nap in the shade. But he had given his brothers and their wives a terrible fright. Rufus would have to be put away, his brothers told their mother. He would have to be taken to the insane asylum.

Never. As long as she lived, said Mrs. Alexander, Rufus would never leave her side. Not once in his life had he disobeyed her; never had he been anything but gentle. How would any of them like it, she wanted to know, if they were teased and attacked by a bunch of impudent snips? No, if anyone was coming to take Rufus away, they were coming over her dead body.

And there the matter rested. The three sons refrained from saying what they foresaw. They foresaw the day when their mother would die and Rufus would be whisked off to Rochester.

After the upheaval of that Saturday afternoon, Mrs. Alexander no longer left Rufus at the pool hall, for it was card-playing Lester who had been the first to speak about putting him away. In my father's keeping, then, Rufus was placed each week without fail. Now and then I would glance up from my work and see him there and wonder how it would end. Morons, according to Miss Sylvestri, sometimes died young. Maybe his mother would survive him, and wouldn't that be a blessing? His brothers' secret intention—like all secrets in Plum—had become public knowledge, and I didn't see how Rufus, after all these years of fixed habits and mother love, could adapt himself to the gruesome life of the asylum, particularly now that he had exhibited strong emotion. Hearing of his anger at the picnic, I now suspected that Rufus was capable of perceptions and emotions beyond what my father and I (and probably most of the village) had formerly believed. Now, though his eyes were consistently shallow and his grin steady, I had a hard time thinking of him in only two dimensions. This was a man who knew things, who felt things, I told myself, and therefore if he outlived his mother he was bound to come to grief. I didn't ask my father what he thought about this. I was afraid he would agree.

In the autumn of my junior year, Mrs. Alexander died. Rufus apparently didn't recognize death when he looked it in the face, for although the coroner said she had been dead since midnight, it wasn't until the following noon that Rufus went next door and by his moaning and wild look alerted Mrs. Underdahl. No one could say for certain how Rufus, waiting for his mother to wake up, had spent the forenoon, but judging later by the evidence and what we knew of his habits, the village imagined this:

Rufus got out of bed on his own and went into his mother's room to see why she hadn't awakened him, why she hadn't started breakfast. The depth of her sleep puzzled him. He was capable of a number of things; he could dry dishes and dress himself, but he couldn't figure out why his mother lay so late in bed. He put on his clothes and breakfasted on biscuits and milk (or rather cream, for he opened a full bottle and swigged off the top) and he evidently passed the rest of the time listening to the radio. In my mind's eye I see him sitting in his favorite chair by the window, soothed by the voice of Arthur Godfrey. I see him grinning when the audience laughs and grinning when it doesn't. At noon he went back into his mother's bedroom and pulled her by the arm, and when she didn't respond, he tugged harder. He pulled her out of the bed and onto the floor. Then, seeing her there at his feet, twisted among the sheets, he perceived something new. A door in his dense thinking opened on an emotion he had never felt before. Not anger this time, but fear. He went straight to Mrs. Underdahl's house and called up the same belching groan he had uttered at the picnic. His great blue eyes were rolling, Mrs. Underdahl later told my father in the store, as though he sensed that this day marked the end of his childhood and now, in his late thirties, he would have to face the world alone—far off from his mother's house, which had been arranged to fit so well his simple needs, far off from his mother's love.

I was one of the altar boys at Mrs. Alexander's funeral. I looked for Rufus among the mourners, but he wasn't there. I supposed, correctly, as it turned out, that he had already been taken to Rochester. At the cemetery it rained. There were dozens of Alexanders standing three-deep around the grave. The little cousins, wearing short pants and neckties, were as antic as ever. While the priest blessed the grave and read aloud the prayers of burial, the cousins shrieked and played tag among the tombstones. Impudent snips, their grandmother had called them.

Six months later my classmates and I were bussed to Rochester for our second look at the unfortunates. Over the years I have tried to figure out why everyone who went through school in Plum during the Lance-Sylvestri era was twice required to pass through this gauntlet of retarded and insane humanity. Surely all of us had been sufficiently impressed the first time by the smells and vacant faces of this dismal congregation, sufficiently impressed by our own good luck at having been spared. One thing we did learn this second trip—and this may have been the lesson our teachers had in mind (particularly Mr. Lance, who taught it by example)—was how to look impassive in the face of chaos. I had the same pain in my stomach that I had two years earlier, and one of the inmates leaped at me and tried to pull off my jacket, but, like most of my classmates, I played the stoic from the time I entered the broad front door until I departed. I acted this way because I was six- teen, the age when nothing seems quite so crucial—espe- cially if freshmen are watching you—as appearing to be above it all; nothing seems quite so clever—if joking would be out of place—as disdain. I discovered that I could be really quite good at looking neutral. The trick was simply to tell myself that none of these crouching, drooling, gawking people were experiencing the misery that visitors pitied them for. They had no knowledge—no memory—of life as it was lived among the normal—life, say, in Plum. Unaware of any better form of existence, they were content. Brainless, they possessed the peace that passes understanding.

But then I saw Rufus. We were boarding the bus when Miss Sylvestri suddenly pointed behind us at the broad front door and said, "Why, that's Rufus Alexander." I turned and saw two men on the doorstep with their backs to us. One was an orderly, the other was a tall, white-haired man with a straight spine and his hands clasped behind his back. It was Rufus, all right, and I was surprised—not only because his hair had turned white, but because he had slipped my mind over the winter; I had forgotten that he lived here now. Where had he been during our tour? Outside, strolling the grounds? Or had he been present in one of the crowded wards we passed through, and had a familiar face told him that we were the Plum delegation? Had he tried to follow us out to the bus? The orderly had him tightly by the elbow and was steering him through the door we had just come out of, but he seemed reluctant to go. Though he didn't struggle, there was a hint of unwillingness in his movements, a hesitation in his step.

This time Miss Sylvestri did not lecture us as Mr. Lance started the bus, but she sat visiting with Pearl Peterson in the front seat on the driver's side. I sat in the back, next to a window, and looked straight at Rufus. The broad front door was now locked and he was standing behind the glass. Our two windows were scarcely thirty feet apart. He didn't look as healthy as he used to. The color was gone from his face and his ledgelike brows were sharper, deeper. While the whiteness of his hair was alarming (in six months it had grown much whiter than his mother's had been), the astonishing thing was the look on his face. He wasn't grinning. His face, without a grin, was that of a much older man, the jaw hanging slack, the cheeks hollow. In his round blue eyes, without a grin, there was something obviously very deep, like yearning. Obvious to me, at least, because his eyes were aimed directly at mine—not slightly above me, the way he used to look at things—and they told me that he had indeed tried to follow us out to the bus; moreover, they told me that mine was the face that reminded him of Plum. I looked away, Mr. Lance shifted gears, and I never saw Rufus again.

ANNIVERSARY

I AM HOME from the drugstore with the Sunday paper and a dozen ballpoint pens, all of them red. I leave the paper in the living room for Donna, and I am halfway up the stairs to my den when I suddenly realize that today is an anniversary. I return to the kitchen and pour two glasses of sherry. On this date ten years ago, my wife and I and eleven hundred others filed into the University of Minnesota football stadium and were given, with a full measure of blessings and addresses, our degrees. We both were twenty-two at the time. The principal speaker was a bishop who said that life was short.

Carrying the two wineglasses, I step out the back door into the sunshine. Robbie, eight, is golfing across the lawn with my putter, digging up grass as he goes along.

Donna is on her knees in the garden, loosening the soil around the rosebushes.

"What? Ten years?" says Donna. "I can't believe it." She smiles and sits back on her heels and takes the glass in her large, dirty garden glove. As we toast a number of things, including my ten years as a high-school teacher, a warm June breeze stirs her red hair and uncovers at the temples a trace of gray. Life is short, said the bishop.

"We will go out to dinner," I announce. "After I finish my schoolwork, you and Robbie and I will go someplace for a festive dinner."

"Don't tell me you're planning to spend the day in the den," says Donna. "Sunday is no day for correcting papers."

"Final grades are due in the office tomorrow morning. My briefcase is full of the scraps of the school year. Odds and ends."

We toast odds and ends; then Donna picks a blossom from the Flaming Peace rosebush and hands it to me. It has a long, thorny stem. Robbie joins us and I give him a sip of sherry, which he spits on the grass.

"Make reservations for three at some fancy place," I tell Donna. "We're stepping out when my work is done."

Upstairs in my den, I set the bottle of sherry on the windowsill and I hang the rose by its thorns in the burlap draperies. It is a small blossom, unfurling from a tomato-colored bud. My window overlooks the garden, and as I crank it open Donna calls up to me, "Promise you won't be up there for the rest of the day."

I have never known Donna to be jealous of another woman, but I have at times a great appetite for solitude, and she is jealous of this room in which I find it. Once while working on my thesis, I spent fourteen days and nights in here emerging only for sandwiches and a bath or two, and she never got over it. She said life was passing me by. And one day last winter, designing a new syllabus, I came in here and worked for twenty-two straight hours, and she broke down and wept. She said her mother had warned her about men who were consumed by their work.

I settle into my deep leather chair and open my briefcase. It is full of quizzes, exams, themes, term papers, and office mail—everything I was too busy to read when it first crossed my desk at school. Some of it goes back several months. I reach in and pull out a paper at random. It is an essay by Becky Burke titled "My Father."

Becky writes with a backward slant and she misspells all but the simplest words. She says here that she loves her father. "He has old fashion ideas," she writes, "and he argues with the length of my skirts but he is patient and he has a sence of humer." She tells of how he used to take her every summer to a "rodio." But now her father is not well. He has been in the hospital for six weeks. Becky fears he will die.

I want to write something tender in the margin, but if I am to read everything in my briefcase this afternoon, I must be off to a quick start. With my red pen I write, "Proofread!" across the top of the paper, and I give her a C. By English Department standards a C is too generous for spelling like Becky's, but I cannot give a girl with a dying father a D.

A sudden cold wind springs through the window, billowing the draperies. Clouds cover the sun and the room darkens. Cranking the window shut, I see a flock of geese flying south—the wrong direction for June.

Next I read a letter from Dale Wood, president of the teachers' union. He wants me to serve for a year as union griever. Although I pay my dues, I am not much of a union man. I lost my enthusiasm years ago when the union went to court to defend a junior-high drama coach who undressed on stage. (Academic freedom, claimed the union; but the judge said nonsense and sent the drama coach somewhere for observation.) Yet Dale Wood has been a friend of mine for a long time. When we golf together he tells hilarious stories. In the margin of the letter I print, in red: "Okay, one year only."

My red ink does not glisten as it should. I try the other pens I bought this morning, but none is any fresher. I have been sold a dozen dry pens. In my desk I have blue and black pens, but I will not use them. In my ten years of teaching I have learned to understand the power of red ink. Red is alarming, decisive. Red puts everything else in the background. When I hand back a student's paper my red ink leaps out at him, and everything he wrote in blue ink has turned insignificant, powerless, faint. Red has the same effect with letters and memos. When I print my response in red it looks, no matter how innocuous the words, like a shout. If I leave my mark in this world, it will be a red mark. Red has force. But today my lettering is pale. It seems to fade before my eyes.

The wind grows stronger. Donna calls to me from the bottom of the stairs. She says she is going to take Robbie to his driving lesson and they will return in an hour. For a moment I am puzzled. Robbie is eight; he does not drive. She must mean she is taking him to the driving range. She must be bored.

"It's awfully windy for driving golf balls," I call to her, but she is gone. I hear the car drive away.

Another letter. This one too is from Dale Wood. Is this his idea of a joke? He writes, "You have doubtless received a letter of official thanks from the union office, but let me add my personal note of gratitude for the way you handled your job as griever these past several years. I know it's never an easy job. . . ." My pen is poised but I can think of nothing to print in the margin. Sometimes Dale tries too hard for a joke. There is nothing harder to respond to than a poor joke. I set this letter aside.

Next in my brief case I find an ad from the publishers of my American-literature text. It says that the new edition, soon to appear, will contain nothing earlier than *Leaves of Grass. Walden* will be replaced by a report from the National Ecology Council, and *Huckleberry Finn* by an assortment of comic strips. The book is to be called *Superlit.* I write "Supertrash" across the ad and drop it in the wastebasket. I pour myself another glass of sherry. It is the color of a rosebud, and smooth.

Donna calls up the stairs: "I am not feeling well." Her voice is husky.

"Are you back already?" I ask.

"I believe I'll lie down."

"Fine, Donna. Lie down. Where is Robbie?"

"Rob is over at Angeline's. I'm sure I'll be all right if I lie down."

"Angeline's? Who is Angeline?"

There is a trace of steam on the window. I wipe it

off and look down at the garden. The Flaming Peace petals are drifting to the ground. Well, it has never been a hardy bush. To get it started, Donna nursed it through four summers without blossoms, and to this day it is easily discouraged by a sudden cold snap or a sharp wind.

I resume reading. This is Alvin Turvig's essay on "Memories." Who is Alvin Turvig? I have never heard of Alvin Turvig. He writes, "My earliest memory is of my family watching, on TV, American troops invading Panama." I read no further. In red I print, "Yours must be the shortest memory in Adams High School," and I move on.

Here is a letter from Cletus Hamsun, who sells insurance in St. Paul. Cletus is the only college classmate I still correspond with. In this letter he seems to be straining, like Dale Wood, to make a joke. He says that he is retiring from the insurance business. He says that he and his wife from now on will spend their winters in El Paso. "Why don't you and Donna join us?" he writes. As I said before, a poor joke leaves me with no reply. I put a red question mark in the margin.

I take a sip of sherry and feel hairs or threads on my lip. Holding the glass up to the light, I pick from the rim the strands of a cobweb. There are raindrops on the window. Outside, a robin with an ebony eye stands on an elm twig, glancing nervously about him at the leaves shaken by the rain. The leaves of the tree are yellow. Can my elm be dying?

Another paper, this one by Peter Turvig. *Peter* Turvig? Who are these Turvigs? He writes, "My Uncle Alvin, who can remember all the way back to the early '70s, is home on vacation. Yesterday he taught me how to fix the brakes on my bike. He goes back to work next week. He is on the staff of the U.S. Embassy in the Republic of Antarctica." This is nonsense. This is fiction written by an imposter. In red I write, "Who are you?"

Rain streams down the window. Here is another letter from Cletus Hamsun. It was mailed in Texas. It has a black border, and it reads, "Sorry to hear about Donna. All the more reason for you to join us in El Paso."

Daylight is fading. I open a letter from someone named Angeline. The envelope is scented.

> *Dear Dad,*
>
> *We are settled at last in a house of our own, with a guestroom ready for you whenever you want to use it. I know how lonely you must be, all by yourself.*
>
> *Rob has been given a nice raise, but I think he is working too hard. I tell him if he isn't careful, life will pass him by. He sends his love.*

My strength drains suddenly away. With great effort I brush the perfumed letter off my lap, and it falls to the floor and lies among a scattering of dusty rose petals as the rain, turning to sleet, hits the window with a ping.

WINNING
SARAH SPOONER

BECAUSE COAXING vegetables out of her immense sandy garden took most of her time in fair weather, Sarah Spooner found widowhood tolerable in the summertime. Like a mother hurrying to her nursery, Sarah, sixty-eight and childless, went straight to her garden first thing after dressing each morning and put the night's growth in order. On the pea vines new tendrils nodded about in the morning breeze, feeling for their makeshift trellis of sticks and strings; on the tomato plants new shoots, tiny and superfluous, needed pruning; and invariably a spear of quackweed had to be carefully extricated from the root of a bean. Only after this preliminary tidying-up did Sarah feel she could afford time for breakfast. Then later, before and after the heat of the day, she hoed and watered until the garden was satisfied. Her

life was so full from April to October that now and then a day would pass in which she forgot to think of the death of her husband Byron.

Then along came winter. Nothing seemed to need her care, except the wintering birds outside her kitchen window, where earlier Byron Spooner had erected his homemade birdfeeder, a combination of plywood and paint resembling a miniature carousel. Now the plywood was curled and the paint faded, but servings of seed and suet were as bountiful as ever, and the new generation of birds as hungry as the last. Sparrows and chickadees were the steadiest visitors, nervously alighting and hopping and scattering the seed and flying away, then returning a moment later, having forgotten to eat. Jays came in pairs, bright blue and hostile, pecking alternately at the seed and at the chickadees. Fat and furry grosbeaks came in orange and yellow flocks of two dozen or more, prolonging their meals by resting between courses in the leafless cotton-wood tree nearby, deliberately tasting, judging, and digesting. These grosbeaks were unpredictable; they might disappear for a week and then return to the cotton-wood early one morning and stay till dusk, by which time Sarah recognized them one from another no matter how they might hop from twig to twig when she wasn't looking.

But feeding a bird was not like raising a pumpkin. Gardening was a calling, watching birds merely a diversion. So, in an attempt to fill up the blank white hours of her first lonely winter, Sarah borrowed her first book from the municipal library, a novel by Thomas Hardy. She read at her kitchen table, which was pushed up against her kitchen window, and although facing the window on sunny days made the printed page uncomfortably bright to the eye, it allowed her to oversee the activity in the bird-feeder. Thomas Hardy carried Sarah away to the cities and the countryside of England, where she was unfamiliar with the landmarks, but not with the people. Often with the shadows of birds crossing the page and seeming to punctuate the passage she was reading, she would straighten up on her straight kitchen chair and speak. "You have known his kind in Gunnars Bluff," she would tell herself, "and now he turns up in Christminster." Or, reminded of her girlhood on the farm, she might say, "You thought she was like someone you knew in country school, and now you remember: it was Otis Hayward's sister; she had the same way about her."

Sarah Spooner's house was old and crooked, with ill-fitting doors and bare light bulbs hanging from the ceilings of narrow rooms. It was one of five houses that stood in a tight row on narrow lots looking dismally across the street at a long windowless wall of the canning factory. Byron Spooner had bought the house when its floors were level and his factory wages were steady. They had planned to buy a better place in their old age, but Byron's susceptibility to pneumonia deprived him of many paychecks over the years, and Sarah was satisfied to remain in the narrow house, especially when she considered the years she had spent converting the scrubby back yard into a garden.

The house next door, the worst of the five, had been occupied for a short time by a young couple with a baby. Sarah had once tried to make their acquaintance. She had gone to their backdoor with six fresh-baked buns and knocked several times. Getting no response, she entered the lean-to porch and opened the kitchen door. The baby, bibbed for a meal at mid-afternoon, was asleep in the highchair, his face resting on the tray in a pile of oyster crackers. As Sarah called, "Anybody here?" she noticed a burner on the gas range was blue with a small flame. She set the buns on a table and stepped around the highchair to the stove.

"Never mind," said a voice.

Sarah looked through the narrow living room and saw the baby's father in pajamas standing in a bedroom doorway.

"I brought over some buns and I noticed your stove was turned on."

The baby woke and cried.

"Never mind," said the father.

"It's no trouble at all. Now if you would like me to fix the baby's bottle . . ."

"I said never mind!" He advanced. "Now get out of here!"

Sarah left in a dither and never went back, but she watched the house closely and learned that the wife worked while the husband stayed home and neglected the child. Then one evening the three of them drove off with all of their belongings in the back of a pickup, and the old bachelor Emmett Heed moved in.

Sarah put Emmett Heed out of her mind, because her last attempt at neighborliness had been such a failure. Besides, if they were to become acquainted it was fitting that Mr. Heed initiate the meeting. And there was little chance of his doing that, for he never stayed home. He spent his days uptown, where he sat on the wooden bench in front of the post office with another retired farmer, and he took his meals at the counter in Lester's Pool Hall.

"How does Mr. Heed appear to you?" Sarah asked herself one snowy morning as she caught a glimpse of him leaving his house. "Dirty," she answered, and turned back to her reading.

In February, midway through her fourth Hardy novel, Sarah developed headaches that blossomed from a small bud at the back of her head in the late afternoons. She endured them through two more novels before she visited a doctor. The doctor said she needed glasses and prescribed a pair that made her dizzy and gave her a pain in the forehead. When she took them back, the doctor charged her nothing for predicting she would feel better when she got used to them. But she never did. April came and drew her away from Thomas Hardy and headaches and into the back yard. She planted her potatoes on Good Friday.

On the Fourth of July Emmett Heed stayed home, for his companion on the wooden bench, Old John Olson, was away visiting relatives and Lester's Pool Hall was closed for the holiday. Emmett sat on his front step looking at the factory wall until the morning sun grew hot, then he moved to the shade of his back yard, where through his overgrown lilac bushes he heard a conversation Sarah Spooner was having with a bird.

The bird was an oriole sitting high in the cottonwood between Emmett's house and Sarah's, and its brimming song was interrupted twice by the blast of a firecracker somewhere in the neighborhood. At both blasts the bird stopped its song for several seconds and Sarah looked up from her garden into the tree, the second time saying, "It's only a firecracker. No harm."

The oriole resumed its song and Sarah turned back to her hoeing, still talking to the bird.

"You should have heard the way it used to be. There were firecrackers all over town in the old days. You would hear them morning till night on the Fourth of July." She straightened up to look at the bird again. "Birds in those days never left off their singing for firecrackers."

True, thought Emmett Heed, there used to be more firecrackers. As for the birds, I doubt if she knows what she's talking about.

On an impulse he rose from his rusty lawn chair and walked through the bushes. He stood at the edge of Sarah's garden and said before she knew he was there, "It's the Fourth of July and I see your corn is knee-high."

Sarah dropped her hoe and turned. "Oh," she said with one hand on her heart and the other brushing wisps of white hair out of her face. "You startled me."

"I'm sorry," said Emmett, wishing he had stayed behind his bushes. He was suddenly conscious of his bare feet and his dirty shirt, originally a pajama top, unbuttoned halfway down his sunken chest. "I'm Emmett Heed." He could think of nothing else to say.

"I'm Sarah Spooner." She picked up her hoe and came down the row between the corn and potatoes. "I declare, if it doesn't rain soon my corn will stay knee-high all summer."

"Out north of town where I had my farm, folks used to pray for rain," said Emmett. "Unless, of course, it rained. In that case they prayed for it to let up."

"Don't you believe in prayer, Mr. Heed?"

"No." Emmett scanned the cottonwood for the oriole that was singing steadily. "It ain't reliable."

"I made lemonade this morning. Will you have a glass, Mr. Heed?"

"Thank you." Emmett was about to follow Sarah into her kitchen when he realized he wasn't invited. "I'll get my lawn chair." he said.

"Put it under the cottonwood," said Sarah from her kitchen door.

Emmett tugged at his rusty chair and brought it under the tree with difficulty, for it was the heavy iron kind. He panted and shakily buttoned his shirt while he waited for Sarah to join him.

She brought a tray with lemonade and six buttered buns. Next she brought out a kitchen chair, and they sat in the shade near the birdfeeder, neglected for the summer.

Emmett's false teeth clicked as he ate five buns and drank most of the lemonade. They talked at length of their common acquaintances, all of whom were dead. Emmett chuckled about the homely Waylander sisters, whose brash attempts at snaring husbands came to nothing, in spite of the prosperous farm they inherited. They went spinsters to their graves.

"It was a sad life they led, Mr. Heed. Have you no pity?"

"Pity?" Emmett craned his neck, looking for the oriole. "I guess not."

"And have you no pity for Herman Waylander, their brother?"

"I don't remember any Herman Waylander. What happened to him?"

"Herman married a woman not suited for him. Some said he should never have married at all, much less a woman so unsuitable."

"No, I don't remember any Herman Waylander." Emmett chewed thoughtfully. "I've always believed some men ain't cut out for marriage." He paused, then added, "Myself for one."

"But the pitiful thing about Herman Waylander was how his wife left him for a time and he knew some happiness, and then she returned and, unsuitable as she was, she dogged him to his grave."

"What made her so unsuitable, if you don't mind my asking?"

"She was a bitch, Mr. Heed."

"Oh."

"A couple just like Mr. and Mrs. Herman Waylander turned up in a book I read last winter. Really, Mr. Heed, you should read it. The people in the story were English, but it reminded me so much of Herman Waylander and his wife I couldn't get over it."

Emmett finally spotted the oriole high in the waving boughs.

"I took up reading after Byron died," said Sarah. "It passes the time."

"I had a sister, she read all the time as a kid," said Emmett. "I never saw much use in it myself."

"Mr. Heed, the winters are long."

They talked of winters gone by until the sun uncovered their shady spot and brought them back to the present. Emmett tugged his chair home and Sarah went back to her garden. She stood at the edge, watering it with a hose, while she planned how she might inoffensively offer to do Emmett Heed's laundry. She had never seen a shirt so dirty.

"If only there were someone whose laundry I could take in," she said to Emmett in mid-August when he paid his second visit to the garden, this time to say she might have the coupons from a grocery circular he found at his door. "Washing and ironing. Not a great deal, mind you, but enough to buy garden supplies. Seeds come to quite a little nowadays, and next summer I'll be needing a new hose, and I'm thinking of a little wire fence to keep out the dogs. Now in your case I could do your things each week for fifty cents. Whoever does your things gets more than that, surely."

"Surely," said Emmett, crossing his arms over the soup stains on his sweatshirt.

"That includes your bed linens and your towels. Wrap your laundry in a sheet and bring it over on Sunday evening. I like to get an early start on washday."

Emmett nodded.

"Fifty cents a week, ironing included," said Sarah. "Now bring your chair over under the cottonwood, Mr. Heed. I have some sherbet."

They ate sherbet and cookies in the shade of the tree.

To Sarah's backdoor on Sunday evening Emmett brought a bundle containing two sheets, two towels, underwear, and a shirt, all of it recently purchased after he burned his older, filthier things in the alley.

He was washed and shaven.

"Please come in, Mr. Heed. I've made a pie."

They sat at the kitchen table, and after the pie Sarah

paged through a book with a faded cover as Emmett sipped his coffee and watched the sun go down.

"I went to the library for this book," said Sarah. "It's about a man named Jude and his wife Arabella, and I declare it's the Herman Waylander story all over again. In this part they've just met for the first time. Here's where Jude picks her up for their first outing together."

She made sure Emmett was listening, then she read: "'All the misgivings vanished that had hitherto haunted him. First they clambered to the top of the great down.' What's a down, Mr. Heed?"

Emmett sipped his coffee and shook his head. "I don't know."

"It's in every book I read. An English term, I suppose."

"I suppose."

"Mr. Heed, would you be interested in reading the book? I have it checked out for two weeks."

Emmett took the book and weighed it in his hands. "I never read a book this thick."

"The thicker the better, I've found." Sarah took the plates and forks to the sink.

Emmett examined a page.

"Long sentences," he said.

He read for a minute as Sarah rattled dishes.

"The folks in this book don't talk like folks I know," said Emmett, smoothing a page with the palm of his hand. "Here's a woman says, 'You're ridiculously inconsistent.' Do you know anybody who talks like that?"

"No, I don't believe so, Mr. Heed."

"Neither do I." Emmett rose with the book and went to the door. "When shall I pick up my laundry?"

"Tomorrow afternoon if it's a drying day."

He paused to look at several cards and clippings Sarah had pinned to the wallpaper by the door. One was a prayer for rain, another a prayer for fair weather.

"Thanks for the pie and the book," he said as he left.

AS SUMMER TURNED to autumn, Sarah was occupied with her reaping, canning, freezing, and pickling; and Emmett was busy trading memories, lies, and rumors with Old John Olson.

Emmett and Old John were confident they were correctly going about the business of growing old. As the townsfolk passed up and down Main Street, the two men sat on the sidewalk bench and chuckled together well into October, when their chuckles turned into little clouds of steam. Old John was not always sure what he was chuckling about, for Emmett's mind was quick, but every suppertime as they parted company, both Emmett and Old John were convinced they had had a good time.

Only on the coldest days did Emmett and Old John leave the wooden bench in front of the post office and retreat to the smokey warmth of Lester's Pool Hall, headquarters for the many retired farmers in town. In the pool hall (where the pool table was seldom used, for Lester charged a dime a game) the two major diversions—playing cards and discussing the weather—bored Emmett; and Old John, an unhealthy little man with a wheeze, who came uptown every day rather than stay home to hear his wife complain about her health, avoided the pool hall because he choked on its smokey atmosphere.

Then one dark day in early November, Old John

Olson choked to death on his asthma, and Emmett was grieved. The next day Emmett was restless on the bench and restless in the pool hall. Alone on the bench, he watched people pass and thought up sharp and cynical things to say, but he had no one to say them to. Then at mealtime in the pool hall he studied the players and kibitzers gathered around the card tables, half-heartedly wondering, too, if he could muster up the energy necessary to strike up a friendship. It wasn't easy building a new set of mutual prejudices, enthusiasms, and jokes. His last set was broken up when Old John took his half with him to the grave. On a stool at Lester's counter, spooning lukewarm soup out of a cracked bowl, for the first time in his life Emmett felt his age.

"What if she is a reader?" said Emmett. "At least she can carry on a conversation."

"Who?" asked Lester, who was leaning on the counter watching him eat.

"Never mind," said Emmett.

He paid for his soup and went home. He searched the clutter under his bed, pulled out the book he had borrowed from Sarah, and read the first few pages.

By the time Sarah Spooner had her garden burned off and bedded down under a layer of manure, freeing her to take up her second winter's reading, Emmett Heed had finished the novel under her supervision. Every evening over coffee in her kitchen Emmett reviewed the day's episode and Sarah told him what she made of it, enticing him to read on by hinting at episodes to come.

Emmett read another book, and then a third. November was cold, and he read in his kitchen with the gas oven lit and open. After he got his November gas bill, he turned off the oven and climbed into bed to read under three blankets and an overcoat. He went uptown only for soup and a sandwich at noon, then came home and read until supper, sitting up in bed with his overcoat around his shoulders. With the space heater on high, the temperature in his house remained a constant fifty-eight degrees.

By Christmas Emmett was eating supper regularly at Sarah's. She had told him it was easier cooking for two than for one, and if Emmett would care to buy a pound of hamburger or a chicken once in a while, he could help her dispose of the beans, tomatoes, corn, squash, kraut, potatoes, peas, and pumpkin that stood preserved in her cupboards.

By Christmas, too, Sarah's headaches were back. She had been reading Dickens for a month and the pain blossomed a little more each day. Twice she made an earnest attempt to wear her glasses, and both times she was practically blind with pain. On Mondays when she washed and ironed her clothes and Emmett's and had no time for reading, her head did not ache. One night in January as they sat at the kitchen table after supper, she handed Emmett the book she had been reading.

"I would like you to look at page 241," she said.

He did so, smoothing the page with his palm.

"My reading days are over, Mr. Heed. My eyes resist the printed page. If only there were someone to read to me."

"Are you asking me to read?"

"If you would be so kind."

"But I'm no reader. There's hundreds of words I

can't pronounce. I run across them every day. I skip right over them."

"I do the same, Mr. Heed, and all I ask is that you finish this one book for me. There's barely fifty pages to go."

In a low voice, rumbling with phlegm, Emmett read the fifty pages, stopping now and then for buns and coffee and for Sarah's comments.

"Serves him right," she said about one of the characters as Emmett, near midnight, approached the conclusion.

"Quiet," said Emmett harshly, engrossed in the story.

When he finished the book, Emmett went home to bed and read his latest Hardy novel, some of it aloud, until he fell asleep.

Every winter day thereafter, instead of taking his book to bed after he returned from Lester's at noon, Emmett sat at Sarah's kitchen table and read aloud through the afternoon as she baked and sewed. Because he seldom looked up as he read, Sarah could study him at length as she mended socks and sewed on buttons. Sometimes he read whole chapters without her hearing a word, for she was concentrating on the starched collar and cuffs of the shirt he was wearing, the patch on the sleeve of his sweater, the part in his white hair.

"Mr. Heed," she said one day, "would you care to come over a bit earlier each day and take your noon meal with me? There's no need for you to be always traipsing uptown for lunch."

Emmett nodded and turned a page.

"And why not breakfast, Mr. Heed? I daresay you neglect your breakfast. There's strength in hot oatmeal."

Emmett nodded and read on.

Only a few sparrows hopped up and down the bare twigs of the cottonwood outside the kitchen window, for the chickadees, grosbeaks, and jays had long since despaired of finding seed in Byron Spooner's feeder.

THE LIFE AND DEATH
OF DELANO KLEIN

AS DELANO KLEIN was growing up, his parents and acquaintances (he had no friends) learned to expect the unusual.

When Delano was in kindergarten, he went to a classmate's birthday party and refused to give up the present he had brought, a wind-up motorcycle with a sidecar. He unwrapped it, held it up for everyone to see, kept it beside his plate while he ate cake, and when he was full he wrapped it up again and took it home.

A year and a half later, when the second grade was studying the United States postal system, Delano helped build a cardboard post office that took up half the classroom, and on the day it was Mary O'Reilly's turn to be postmistress (Mary got nothing but A's), he put a hard dog turd in the mailbox.

When he was ten, Delano raised his hand in Sunday School and told the pastor's wife that he planned to give up smoking for Lent.

In his early teens, Delano went on a reading binge that lasted for three years. He read in bed, he read at meals, and on summer afternoons he read in a tree. He disliked people, and he hardly ever spoke, even to his parents. His mother was vexed by his solitary behavior, but his father said, "Never mind."

"But he drives me crazy," said his mother.

"Delano is a born scholar," said his father. "He has a great future ahead of him." This was during the one breakfast each week that Delano's father ate at home. Delano's father was a doctor who made a fortune as the foremost reader of x-rays in two states. He was continually on the move, flying from city to village in his red Cessna, dropping out of the sky to diagnose fractures and tumors at a glance, then soaring off into the haze. He came home once a week and stayed overnight.

"All I know is he drives me crazy," said Delano's mother. "And his pimples are getting worse. Can't you take him with you to Montpelier and get him out of the house for a few days?" Delano was sitting at her left, eating Kix and reading.

"Yes," said the doctor thoughtfully. "He can come with me to Montpelier. I'll take the car and we'll talk." This was the day that Dr. Klein was to fly to Montpelier, then on to Barre, St. Johnsbury, and Franconia; but he was struck now by an unforeseen wave of remorse for all the days he had been away from home—those irrecoverable years, empty (he imagined) of whatever it was that fathers owed their sons. He backed his new avocado Oldsmobile out of the garage and had the gardener dust it off and check the oil while he waited for Delano, who had gone obediently upstairs to his room and was slowly stuffing clothes into a duffel bag, trying to make the job last until he finished the last few pages of the book open on his dresser.

Halfway to Montpelier, the Oldsmobile made an alarming noise under the hood and became suddenly hard to steer. The doctor turned off the highway and into a small town where he found a mechanic. The trouble was a leak in the power-steering hose. The mechanic didn't have a hose to replace it, but he would call Burlington and have one sent out on the noon Greyhound. Standing on the oil-stained drive of the gas station, Doctor Klein took off his tie and pulled his sweaty shirt away from his chest and shaded his eyes from the painful sun that shines on small, dull towns in July. What could he possibly do with himself for two hours? It was no use trying to pass the time with Delano, for the boy had nothing to say. For seventy miles, the doctor had tried to start a conversation, but Delano never once looked up from the book in his lap. The doctor set off down the street, in search of a drink.

Meanwhile, Delano studied the engine of the Oldsmobile. When the mechanic first opened the hood, Delano had stepped out of the car to see what an engine looked like, and he was entranced. He asked the mechanic the name of this hose and that wire, this housing and that lever. When a customer drove into the station for gas, Delano asked and was granted permission to look under the customer's hood. At twelve-thirty when the doctor returned to the station, wilting from too much gin too early in the day, he found his son clamping the new power-steering hose into place. This was the first day of Delano's interest in things mechanical. Until the very end of his life he never read another book.

At eighteen, when most of his fellow graduates from Persons Academy entered college, Delano entered the employment of Hernig and Sons Plumbing, Heating, and Refrigeration. He specialized in refrigeration. He was Hernig's lowest-paid repairman, but in his spare hours he designed an ice-cube freezer that came to be in much demand by bartenders, for it produced forty cubes a minute and was only half the size of other icemakers then on the market.

He called it the Havana Cuber, and soon he was in business for himself, selling and servicing these units in an ever-expanding territory. In his ice-blue van he traveled much the same route that his father flew. Across upper New England he built up a hearty comradeship among bartenders, and his first drink was always on the house.

In Manchester, New Hampshire, one late afternoon, Doctor Klein stepped into a dark bar where Delano was installing a new icemaker. Delano had been living away from home for some time now, and his father could hardly believe that this jovial young man, joking with the waitress as he worked, was his son. He ordered a drink and watched him from a distance. When Delano finished installing the machine and sat at the bar, the doctor went up to him and put his arm around his shoulders and said, "My son." Delano turned cold. The doctor made a dozen pleasant remarks, but for all the response he got from his son, he might have been speaking Chinese. After one drink together, the doctor left in anguish and Delano moved to a booth where he and the waitress cuddled and got drunk.

And eventually they got engaged. Delano, who was twenty-four at the time, and the waitress, whose name was Joylynn, planned to marry on the first Saturday of June. Joylynn quit her job to sew her wedding dress. On the last Saturday of May, Delano called her from Bangor, Maine, and said he changed his mind. He said he hoped this didn't cause her any inconvenience. When Joylynn's father finally traced him down by phone and asked for an explanation, Delano told him that being married wasn't going to lower the cost of his automobile insurance as much as he thought it would.

Throughout the rest of his twenties, visiting bars on business, Delano drank too much. But when he turned thirty, he quit drinking altogether and fell in love with a dental assistant who had passable good looks and an earnest faith in God. She was small and calm and her name was Ernestine.

Delano turned his icemakers over to a distributor, keeping half interest in the profits, and he married Ernestine. They settled down on a farm near Ashby, New Hampshire, because Ernestine had always dreamed of living in the country. Delano didn't like farming, but he didn't have to, for the Havana Cuber was going strong nationwide. In a short time, without doing anything, he was making three times as much money as his father.

Ernestine bore two daughters, and Delano came to be what is known as a good family man. He took his wife and daughters skiing and hiking, and he loved to see them dressed up in new clothes. Ernestine often spoke about God—a little too often to suit Delano—but he bore her faith patiently.

"Haven't you found your Savior yet?" Ernestine would ask him on Sunday mornings.

"No," he would say.

One summer Delano's father flew into a hail storm over the White Mountains, lost his way, crashed, and died.

After the funeral, Ernestine said, "You really must learn to place your trust in the Lord."

"I suppose," said Delano.

In his middle thirties, Delano was becoming bored. One eternal, rainy afternoon he picked up a novel and began to read, but the story made him yawn and he quit reading on page twelve. He remembered how, in his teens, he had read an average of five books a week. How was that possible? He went to the window and watched the rain fall on his land. He decided that thirty-five was too early in life to be gainfully unemployed. It occurred to him that the knoll at the far end of the pasture was the perfect setting for a large new house. He picked up the phone and called an architect in Boston and told him to design a three-story stone house with a sundeck. When the plans arrived, Delano found an old stonemason in Ashby, and the two of them built the house themselves. It took them six years.

After moving his family across the pasture into the new house, Delano spent weeks walking from room to room, admiring what he had done. He imagined taking guests on a tour of the place, but he and Ernestine never had guests. Every day, he opened every door—the door to the wine cellar, the door to the bathroom closet on the third floor—and he relived the pounding of all the nails, the spacing of all the studs. He had turned the decorating over to Ernestine, and she had kept it plain. Delano suspected that this plainness was due not so much to her good taste as to her lack of imagination, but the result was attractive and comfortable, for the large ascetic rooms were filled on clear days with sunshine and on dark days with flickering orange light from the granite fireplaces.

But how much of his life can a man spend admiring his house? Delano, at forty-two, was bored again. He phoned the old stonemason in Ashby and asked him to come out for a tour of the house, but the stonemason said he was busy. It was January, and it was snowing. He chose at random a volume from the bookcase and sank into a chair to read. It was an old textbook of Ernestine's (she had spent three semesters in college) and there fell from between its pages a poem she wrote when she was nineteen. "The Voices of God," it was called.

> *When I want to know what God is thinking,*
> *I scatter seed and meal on the snow*
> *And listen to the small noises of the gathering chickadees,*
> *The sharp shrieks of the jays;*
> *Or I wake at night to hear the clock,*
> *The tick and the tock.*

Delano liked the poem. He liked it so much, in fact, that he was overcome by an unfamiliar emotion, which he guessed was tenderness. He paged through the book—a literature anthology—then he read the poem again. He found more textbooks. For the first time since the power steering failed in his father's car on the way to Montpelier, he felt the urge to read. He examined the books. Here was a survey of American history a man might do well to study. Here was a psychology text with chapters on kleptomania, dipsomania, and frigidity. Wouldn't it be good to learn the reasons people acted so funny? Here was a physics book with a long unit devoted to, of all things, refrigeration. And he found four more poems by Ernestine. Delano didn't know much about poetry, but he knew what he liked. He wondered if he could learn to write a poem. He picked up the phone and called Plymouth State College and said he wanted to enroll as a freshman. The registrar signed him up for three classes on the spot.

Ernestine was thrilled.

"I'm not promising anything," Delano told her. "I'll commute for a term and see how I like it. If I like it—who knows—we may move to Plymouth and I'll major in physics."

"You'll like it just fine," said Ernestine.

Delano liked it just fine. His three courses were physics, introduction to psychology, and American literature. One day after class, he showed his literature instructor a poem.

"I thought I'd try my hand," he said. "It might be a rotten poem, but I'd like to know what you think."

The instructor said it was really quite good, and he encouraged Delano to write another. The instructor thought, but did not say, that the poem revealed a depth of soul he had overlooked in Delano.

By the end of the term, Delano had handed in a total of five poems. One afternoon in May, the instructor wrote a page of comments, clipped it to the five poems, and gave them back to Delano.

Some people sneeze at the sun, and Delano was one of them. Driving home against the sun that same afternoon, Delano sneezed four times and lost control of his car, which rolled off the highway and dropped into a rocky ditch. Hanging upside-down in his seat belt—his neck broken—Delano died.

The funeral was small, and nobody could think of much to say. The preacher said Delano was a good man, and the distributor of the Havana Cuber agreed. The old stonemason, who knew him as well as anyone because they had worked side by side for six years, stood at the edge of the group and tried to draw some sort of conclusion from the life and death of this man, some generality about the human condition; but his thoughts were interrupted by Delano's mother, who, coming away from his coffin, said she was glad to see that Delano's acne hadn't been permanent.

Among the effects taken from the wreckage, and delivered to Ernestine by a highway patrolman, were the five poems with the page of comments. On a hopefully sunny day after the funeral, when her daughters were back in school and Delano's mother was on her way home, Ernestine went out on the sundeck overlooking the sloping pasture and sat down to read the poems. A pair of blackbirds pecked in the grass beneath her, clucking like hens. The sky was blue-white, the color of thin milk.

When Ernestine read the instructor's remarks, her heart leapt. The instructor said that the poems manifested a serene depth of soul, a sensitivity to nature, and a faith in God.

So it had come to pass, after all, thought Ernestine. Delano had finally put his trust in the Lord. How like him not to have told her. Why had he not told her? Ernestine wept for sorrow and she wept for joy.

She turned the page and read the first poem. *When I want to know what God is thinking*, it began, *I scatter seed and meal on the snow, and listen to the small noises of the gathering chickadees.*

The rest of the poems, too, were hers.

DODGER'S RETURN

ROSS LOVES his class reunions. So much comes back. His school days (mostly lackluster while he lived them, mostly tedious) return to him once every ten years in the high colors and rich distortions of memory. Since breakfast Ross and his wife Martha have driven two hundred miles for this reunion, and tonight, entering the Willowby Country Club, Ross is dazzled by the sight of his forty classmates. At their ten-year reunion most of these people were changing jobs. At their twentieth, spouses. This time they seem to have decided to change their looks. Old friends advance upon Ross in shapes and clothes none of them could have foreseen in high school. A lot of the men are trying out the shaggy hairstyles of their children; a few, no hair at all. The women look smart and a bit stiff, speaking fluently through their smiles as they size each other up.

"Relax," Martha whispers wisely into Ross's ear after he's had several drinks and a dozen high-pitched conversations. Martha, who knows how worked up Ross gets over life stories (his own and others') can read his blood pressure in the capillaries of his nose. Martha herself graduated from a city school in a class of 800; she and Ross have gone to only one of her reunions, and Martha insists that they will go back for only one more—her fiftieth. She says it's excusable to get emotional over your tenth and your fiftieth, but those in between are meaningless. How typical of Martha to calculate her feelings ahead of time. She often has to remind Ross that it's the mesh of their contrasting temperaments (his feverish; hers unruffled, resolute) that has made their marriage so durable.

Dinner settles Ross down. For one thing, a lot of his excitement is drained off in the effort it takes to chew the gristly underdone ribs. For another, sitting next to him at the banquet table is Charles Bohannon, a classmate he never knew very well. Why couldn't Ross have been placed within talking distance of Bruce Romberg or Lanny Mulligan or one of the Crowninshield twins or any of the other men he used to play football with? Or next to Pearl Peterson, with whom he used to compete (during his studious phases) for the highest grades? These people and others like them, including Ross, had been the inner circle of this class—the achievers, the standouts, the most likely to succeed. Whenever he called up memories of his schoolmates, it was this class within a class that came to mind—not the likes of Charles Bohannon, who instead of going out for sports always hurried straight home from school to help out his father in the dray business.

"I've got a fleet of eight trucks now," says Bohannon, pushing away his plate and searching his pockets for a smoke. "We haul cattle to St. Paul, grain to Duluth." Bohannon's bald head is flat and very shiny. He looks more like an accountant than a trucker. He wears oversize glasses with oval lenses that nearly touch the corners of his mouth. In his checkered sport coat he finds a pair of cigars with plastic mouthpieces and offers one to Ross. Ross declines. Bohannon lights up and says, "I'll bet you don't remember Dodger Hicks."

"My God, Dodger Hicks—my first friend in this town!" Ross is plunged suddenly back to the autumn when he was ten—1943, the year he and his father and mother moved to Willowby from Minneapolis, Ross a fifth grader, his parents the new owners of the Willowby Grocery. "I don't believe Dodger's name has ever come up at one of these reunions. He was the first criminal I ever knew—the *only* criminal, come to think of it."

"Dodger lived here in Willowby only two years," says Bohannon, his fumy cigar clenched in his teeth. "He and his mother came to town about a year before you did, and they moved away toward the end of the fifth grade. He spent most of his teenage years in the reformatory—I suppose you knew that."

"Yes. And I heard somewhere—or did I read it?— that he's been in and out of prison ever since."

Bohannon—leaning away from Ross and toward Mrs. Bohannon, who is telling him something in his far ear—nods and says, "Mostly *in*. Armed robbery."

Dodger Hicks. Ross's recollection of Dodger is at once old and fresh. Some memories grow mindworn from standing, like shopworn merchandise, too long on display; but for over a third of a century the memory of Dodger has lain largely undisturbed in the protective tissue of Ross's subconscious, and now, drawing it out, he finds the images clear and vital. Dodger's sallow face. Dodger's wide cheekbones. His manner of nodding his head when he spoke and his manner, when spoken to, of squinting and showing his teeth. Dodger was twelve and taller than the rest of the fifth graders, having taken three tries (somewhere afar, not in Willowby) to pass from the first grade to the second. A poor reader, he was frequently taunted for what his classmates thought was stupidity. At recess he lingered, unwelcome, at the edges of games. His pale hair hung unevenly about his head—cut by Dodger himself, using one of the small, dull scissors from art class. He had no father.

Pushing himself back from the banquet table, Ross lowers his head, four knuckles to his brow, and delves further into this layer of memory. He visualizes his first day of school in Willowby. Down a street of strangers he walked to school in the rising warm sun of early September. The moment he set foot in the fifth grade, Dodger, as though lying in wait, became his friend. He probably *had* been lying in wait, for it soon became apparent to Ross that Dodger was utterly without companionship, the parents of Willowby having warned their children away from him because he stole things from stores—crayons, comic books, candy. He was surely a pioneer shoplifter in that day and age. But Dodger, though a budding kleptomaniac, had a heart like Robin Hood's. Upon meeting Ross for the first time, Dodger gave him a stick of grape gum (the crumbly gum of wartime) stolen from the Willowby Grocery.

After school that day, Dodger went home with Ross to look over his belongings. Ross's parents were working at the store; the house was empty. This was a high, gabled house with a dirt street at its front door, a farmer's field at its back. They climbed the stairs to Ross's room, where Dodger, taking inventory, rummaged through a box of castoff toys in the closet. He drew out a boomerang, a heavy, beautifully curved piece of laminated wood, thick at the middle and tapering at the ends. A Christmas gift from an uncle, this boomerang had never interested Ross; it returned to the thrower only if the thrower had a stronger arm than Ross's. Dodger had never seen a boomerang. "What is it?" he asked, hefting it, turning it over delicately in his hands, obviously pleased with its smooth lines. Dodger's fingers were long and sensitive, the tools of petty larceny.

"You grab it by one end and throw. It's supposed to come back."

"Let's try it," said Dodger, nodding eagerly.

"No, some other time, when my dad's home. He has to throw it for me."

"Maybe *I* could throw it for you."

"No, you need a lot of room to make it work."

Dodger pointed out the window at the farmland stretching to the horizon. "More room than that?"

Ross had momentarily forgotten that behind this house lay whole counties of open prairie. In the city his father had had to drive him to a high school football field to show him how the boomerang worked. "All right," said

Ross, "see for yourself." They went downstairs and out the back door.

The field bordering the back yard had produced something of early harvest—peas perhaps, or onions—and had already undergone its fall plowing. The furrows were deep and moist. Dodger carried the boomerang to the edge of the field, drew back his right arm, kicked up his left foot, and accomplished a magnificent throw—all on sheer instinct, apparently, for Ross's only instruction had been to show him where to grip the boomerang. It sailed up and away, spinning as it climbed, and at its apogee— incredibly high and small—it tilted almost vertical as it wheeled around and began its return flight, picking up speed and spinning faster and faster and heading straight for the boys' heads and passing over them as they threw themselves flat and crashing through a kitchen window. At the sound of breaking glass, Dodger was up and running. He never glanced back or said good-bye.

On the second day of school, a day of wind and intermittent rain, Dodger was distant. Ross was grieved, Dodger being his only friend. At recess, as the others chose teams for softball, Ross followed Dodger to the swings and said there was nothing to fear from the broken window. His father had already replaced the glass.

Dodger squinted, lifting his lip. His teeth weren't clean. "No kidding? Didn't you catch heck or nothing?" He looked doubtful, like someone whose errors had always met punishment, never pardon.

"My dad just said to take the boomerang out in the field farther. Come back this afternoon and we'll throw it some more." Ross almost said please.

Dodger nodded, friendship restored. "We'll go to my house first. I've got something for you."

After school they went to the apartment where Dodger lived with his mother. "Ma?" he called as they climbed the stairs, but his mother wasn't home. Dodger showed Ross around: three low-ceilinged rooms containing a hot plate and a toilet, but no sink or refrigerator or bathtub; Dodger and his mother washed in a basin and chilled their milk on a windowsill overlooking a blacksmith shop across the alley. In the sitting room, Dodger opened a drawer of the dresser that stood beside his cot and drew out a cap gun fresh from the Five and Dime, a snub-nosed pistol of heavy steel, a wartime rarity. He said Ross could have it.

Ross took it and admired it. The silvery barrel was untarnished; the crosshatching of the grip was pleasingly rough to his palm; the trigger was stiff. "Thanks," he said.

Dodger nodded, towering over him, admiring it himself. "I'll get you some caps for it tomorrow."

Then they went to Ross's house. They took the boomerang out into the plowed field (the sky was clearing now, but the wind still blew) and Dodger perfected his throwing style. Otherwise ungainly, Dodger handled the boomerang with remarkable grace. At least three times out of four he was able to send it sailing farther than he had the day before. Its return was erratic because of the wind, and as the two boys ran this way and that to retrieve it, the heavy soil built up on their shoes like clogs and they had to pause every few minutes to pare it away, using the edge of the boomerang as a blade.

Ross studied Dodger's delivery. Dodger was throwing

sidearm, with a vigorous snap of his wrist. Ross tried it, but was only half successful. Although the boomerang sailed a good long way, it didn't come back; at the point where it should have made its midair turn, it was already falling to earth.

"Maybe you should try it like a discus," said Dodger, demonstrating how a discus thrower uncoils like a spring before letting go. "You get more power that way."

"Who taught you to throw a discus?"

"Nobody. I saw a guy throw one in a newsreel once."

Good advice: Ross's next throw climbed high into the wind, turned, came back like a shot, and stabbed itself—*chunck!*—into a hummock of wet earth.

At dusk Ross's parents came home from the store and called him to supper. Dodger followed him up onto the back porch, and when Ross slipped off his muddy shoes, so did Dodger.

"Don't you have to go home?" said Ross.

Dodger said he didn't. He went into the kitchen and said hello to Ross's parents, and when Ross's mother invited Dodger to stay for supper, he was already sitting down at the table. After supper the boys played marbles on the living-room rug as they listened to the radio. When it was time for Ross to go to bed, Dodger had to be told to go home.

On the third day of school Ross renounced Dodger. For all his training to the contrary, Ross was no less cruel than the average ten-year-old. He was a heartless opportunist. For two days he had been studying the cliques of the fifth grade, and it struck him that in order to be accepted by his more glamorous classmates—Bruce Romberg,

Lanny Mulligan, Pearl Peterson, the Crowninshield twins—he would have to loosen his ties with Dodger. He suffered a brief pang of conscience, but nothing serious. The temptation to forsake Dodger for a place among the standouts was irresistible. Bruce Romberg and Pat Crowninshield excelled at softball. Lanny Mulligan's father owned a movie theater. Pearl Peterson wore lipstick and claimed to read her mother's book-club novels. Johnny Crowninshield ran faster than anyone else in the fifth grade, and even the sixth. Furthermore, Ross sensed that these achievers, though aloof, had their eye on him. The fifth grade was their island and Ross, like Dodger before him, had been cast up on the beach. The natives were watchful, waiting for a sign. Would they judge him a perpetual outcast, like Dodger, or did he possess the key to their trust?

The key, it occurred to Ross on that third day of school, was his boomerang. Having captured Dodger's fancy, might it not appeal to the inner circle as well? During the noon hour, Ross hurried home for the boomerang, and with five minutes left before class he carried it through the schoolyard and across the street to the high school athletic field. Dodger went with him. First Ross made sure that the students loitering around the school were watching, and then he unleashed what he hoped would be his mightiest throw. Alas, it was one of his worst. In his eagerness he had forgotten to snap his wrist. The boomerang flew scarcely forty yards and fell to the ground like a stick of firewood. Dodger set out to retrieve it, outran Ross, and in a single motion of great beauty, like a dancer's, he picked the boomerang off the grass and sent it flying nearly the length of the football field—eighty yards out and back, his mightiest throw. And his last. Across the street came a multitude that included Bruce, Lanny, and the twins. They shouted and scuffled for a turn with the boomerang. Ross and Dodger stepped aside and watched them experiment with various styles of delivery. Once every five throws, the boomerang returned, but no one's throw matched Dodger's. When the bell rang, Ross was handed the boomerang with respect, and he crossed the street surrounded by new friends who clapped him on the back and called him by name. Bruce and Pat invited him to a high school football game under the lights. Lanny and Johnny invited him to Saturday's Roy Rogers matinee. Ross caught a glimpse of Dodger at the edge of this crowd; he was slouching along with a faint smile on his lips, thinking perhaps that by his skill with the boomerang he had won acceptance along with Ross. But of course he had won nothing of the kind. He was sure to remain an outsider through the rest of the school year, indeed throughout his life, and Ross knew it if Dodger didn't. Ross also knew that his own future lay with the standouts, the athletes, the achievers, and not with this tall, pale lingerer, this squinting, generous thief. Ross had won a foothold on the island, and Dodger, for all Ross cared, could now wash out to sea.

This shift of allegiance wasn't clear to Dodger until later that afternoon when he began once more to follow Ross home, and Ross turned him back. "We can't play together anymore," said Ross, avoiding Dodger's squint. They stood beneath a yellowing elm in front of the school.

"Why?"

"Because." Ross chose not to go into it, chose not to accuse Dodger of being a weight on his rising fortunes, a barrier to his entering the larger world of the inner circle.

"Because why?" The *why* was drawn out, an adenoidal whine.

"Because my folks said so." A lie.

This memory is so painful to Ross (literally painful; he feels throttled, short of breath) that he forces himself to choke it off. He raises his eyes and sheds the image of Dodger and looks about him at the reunion. Several people have left their places at the banquet table and have gone into the bar. At the far end of the room a four-piece band is arranging itself on a platform: electric guitar, saxophone, drums, piano. Two of the musicians are elderly, two are teenagers: impossible to say whether the reunion is in for rock or swing. On Ross's right, Martha, smoking a cigarette, is telling a woman across the table what the League of Women Voters is all about. The woman, freshening her lipstick in a small mirror, doesn't seem to be paying attention. On Ross's left, Charles Bohannon is running the tip of his cigar around the inner rim of an ashtray, carefully peeling off particles of ash as they form. He is saying, "I saw him two summers ago in June. That was the month I painted my house."

"Dodger? You saw Dodger Hicks?"

"Damnedest thing." Bohannon clears his throat and adjusts his glasses. "I was up on a ladder painting the front of the house. The wife and I live in the same house I used to live in as a kid. You remember—the place with the big porch on the east end of Main Street. The wife and I moved in after my folks died. We've lived there eight years now. In another year or two they say the highway will be rerouted to miss town altogether. Which will be nice—then we won't have all that traffic at the front door."

"You actually saw Dodger Hicks?"

"Two years ago in June. I was up on the ladder—a warm day, seventy-five degrees—and I heard this voice behind me. I turned and looked down and there stood Dodger grinning up at me. Or I guess you'd call it squinting. Remember that way he had of squinting? What had it been—thirty-five, thirty-six years?—well, I knew him right off. He'd put on weight, but he was the same old Dodger, same old pasty color, same wide face. I called him by name. 'Hello, Dodger,' I said, 'how you been?' I came down the ladder with my paint bucket in one hand and my brush in the other."

Martha has given up on the League of Women Voters. She leans forward in order to see around Ross and follow Bohannon's story.

"Now here comes the strange part. I no more than set my foot on the ground when Dodger said, 'Let me paint—give me your coveralls.' He took my bucket and brush right out of my hands and he set them on the grass and said again, sort of grufflike, 'Give me your coveralls.'" Here Bohannon sucks on his cigar and waits for Ross to display some sign of amazement.

"I don't think that's so strange. Dodger was always generous."

"Now wait a minute, maybe I'm not making myself clear. Picture it—I came down off this ladder, see, and I was confronted by this ex-con I hadn't seen since grade five, and all he could say was, 'Let me paint—give me your coveralls.' Up close he looked sort of dangerous. His face had pockmarks. To tell the truth he scared the hell out of me. I said, 'Sure thing, Dodger, paint my house,' (here Bohannon works his face into an expression of humble obedience, demonstrating for Ross and Martha how submissive he had been) and I stepped out of my coveralls—I was wearing Bermuda shorts underneath—and I handed them over. They were kind of small for him. He couldn't zip up the front and they bound him in the crotch, but he put them on anyhow and he climbed the ladder and painted my house for about fifteen minutes. Crazy situation— picture it—crazy as hell. He didn't say anything. Just stood up there on the ladder painting, reaching places I hadn't been able to reach. I puttered around down below, scraping a little paint and trying to make conversation, and he never said a word. Then in about fifteen minutes he came down the ladder and handed me my bucket and brush and took off my coveralls, and do you know what he said? He said, 'Thanks.'"

Martha and Bohannon look at Ross for his reaction. He shakes his head, slowly, sadly.

"That's all he said was 'Thanks,' and he set off down the highway, hitchhiking out of town. I saw him get a ride with a farmer I know . . ."

On the bandstand the electric guitar comes to life with a stammering twang, drowning out Bohannon. He shrugs and turns away, indicating that his story was over anyhow. Sax, piano, and drums join in; it takes them a few measures to catch up with the guitar and produce a recognizable melody—a thudding rendition of "Ghost Riders in the Sky." Ross remembers Vaughn Monroe. Martha turns to him, smiling, the tilt of her head meaning *Shall we dance?*

THREE A.M. at the Willowby Motel. Ross lies awake in the moonlit room, his head full of the past, Martha asleep at his side. Instead of his customary post-reunion cheer, he is feeling sad, and it's because of Dodger Hicks. He tries to direct his thoughts away from the fifth grade and focus them on the triumphant years of high school—the conference football championships, the drama club awards—but it's no use; again and again his mind spins back to Dodger, and he is stabbed by regret. He is sure that Dodger's life could have followed a different course had he not turned his back on him that afternoon in 1943. It isn't implausible for Ross to imagine that with one stalwart companion in Willowby, Dodger—a sensitive boy at heart—might have left town with more faith in humanity. A greater capacity for happiness. An awareness that the world's joys were attainable by methods other than pilfering. Aching with guilt, Ross kicks off the blanket and sits on the edge of the bed, an act of such suddenness that it wakes Martha and seems to require an explanation.

He tells her the story of Dodger and their two-day friendship. He describes the parting of their ways under the elm in the schoolyard. He shakes his head in shame, speaking of Dodger's life as a thief and a prisoner. He says he's partially at fault.

"Don't be childish, Ross." Martha, lying on her back, brushes hair from her eyes. "In looking for something to worry about, the fifth grade is off limits to people our age. It's prehistoric."

"But I have this vivid memory of Dodger trying to

follow me home on that third day, and my telling him he was anathema. I was his only hope for companionship and I told him my parents wouldn't stand for it. A horrible lie. And now I recall something else. This happened a few weeks later. My mother and I were in the Five and Dime, shopping, and we met Dodger. My mother said, 'Why don't you come over and see us anymore?' Dodger looked puzzled. He was standing under a display of Halloween masks, obviously trying to figure out if my mother was joking or leading him into a trap. Or whether, by some bit of luck, she had changed her mind about him. But he took no chances, Martha. He never came to see us. Instead, he went into a life of crime."

"God, how melodramatic." Martha covers her eyes with her forearm and gives herself up to a long yawn. Then she says, "If Dodger was gone by the end of the fifth grade, you couldn't possibly have made a difference in his life. You didn't know him long enough. And you admit he was a thief before you ever met him."

"But that was Dodger's watershed year, Martha." Ross goes to the window. Across the highway is a corn field. Above it, all but the biggest stars are obscured by the harsh gleam of the full moon. "You have to understand what Willowby meant to him. Though he came here in the fourth grade and left in the fifth, he obviously continued to think of Willowby as home. Otherwise what was he doing back here two years ago? The way I see it, he came back between prison terms in order to prove to himself that his life had a foundation. There's that longing in all of us, Martha, to go back where we came from."

"There is?"

"He wanted a fresh look at the only community he had ever felt a part of, so he hitchhiked to Willowby and walked up and down Main Street, hoping for that old sense of belonging. I imagine he went into the post office and the Five and Dime and maybe the bowling alley, but chances are he didn't recognize a single face from his boyhood. Chances are he didn't speak to anyone, afraid of verifying that he had made no mark on anyone's memory. So he walked around aimlessly, until he came to this house at the edge of town where he saw a man on a ladder. He knew that this had been the home of Charles Bohannon the boy, and he peered up to see if this was Charles Bohannon the man, and sure enough, it was. He called to him, and he was overjoyed when Bohannon, looking down, said, 'Dodger, how you been?' Bohannon knew him. At last, a link with his past. His life had a foundation after all. Love welled up in his breast. Love for Bohannon. Love for Willowby. He was overcome by an impulse to thank Bohannon, to reward him for remembering him, and so when Bohannon came down the ladder, Dodger said, 'Let me paint,' and he grabbed the bucket and brush— impetuously, I suppose, but meaning to be kind—and he slipped into Bohannon's coveralls and went right to work. That fits his character as I remember it, Martha. He was always generous. He was sensitive."

Martha turns on her side, facing the wall. "Ross, please come to bed."

"But think of my cruelty, Martha." He turns from the window and addresses her moonlit back. "Think what a bastard I was."

"You're forgetting about peer pressure, Ross. To survive

in the fifth grade you had to spurn Dodger. Peer pressure makes bastards out of all of us when we're young, girls even more than boys." Her reply begins as a drone but grows lively as she calls up a recollection of her own: "To get an invitation to my junior prom I had to go steady for a month with a jerk named Albert Edgely." She chuckles.

Ross lights a cigarette and sits in a chair. He feels a bit more at ease now, having aired his guilt. He dwells for a time on a number of other old friends. He thinks about Johnny Crowninshield, how fleet of foot he had been as a boy and what a disappointingly large belly he has developed in his forties. He thinks about Pearl Peterson, who looks less bookish and more vivacious in middle age than she had as a girl. Lanny Mulligan wears a diamond ring on each hand. But soon his thoughts circle back to 1943. He sees his old boomerang with startling clarity; he sees the trademark stamped into the wood—a circle surrounding the stylized figure of a duck in flight. For several months back then, thanks to Ross's example, the most highly prized birthday gifts were boomerangs. Through the autumn of 1943 boys gathered in fields at the edge of town and perfected their delivery. They threw until late November, when the ground became rock-hard with frost and all the boomerangs, Ross's included, developed splintered wingtips and flew like wounded birds. By the following spring the boomerang was out of vogue. But what had made it suddenly so popular? Was it simply the magic of flight, or was there something in the boomerang's trajectory that appealed to the instincts of ten-year-olds? At that age, Ross recalls, he and his contemporaries were beginning to play fast and loose with things they had for-

merly clutched at with desperation—toys, fantasies, parents. Having been graspers for a decade, ten-year-olds
were learning to give, but they gave only with a reward in
view. They loved, but only with the promise of love in
return. Did the boys of Willowby, therefore, see in the
boomerang an emblem of human relationships—the giving
and the getting? When you were skillful, the boomerang—
though cast away—came back, tracing perhaps in its circle
of flight the design of love, as the narrow young mind
conceived of love. Nothing offered without recompense.

Ross is pleased by this thought, this abstraction of
what a few moments ago had been a painful worry. He
relaxes. He looks over at Martha, who appears to be sleep-
ing. With his elbow on the arm of the chair, he moves his
cigarette and its rising smoke in and out of the moonlight,
and he remembers how hard it was for him to give birthday presents in those days. Whenever possible, the gifts he
bore to parties were trinkets he had chosen for their lack of
appeal to himself, and when on occasion he gave away
something he coveted, he consoled himself with dreams of
his own next birthday when he would reap the harvest of
his generosity. He blows gently at the smoke, watching it
rise, and he wonders if he is any more generous as a man
than he had been as a boy. How can he be sure there isn't
still a certain calculation in his giving? He examines his
motives of recent days—the favor he did for a colleague at
the office, the splurging he did on Martha's birthday jew-
elry. He draws no conclusions but grows weary trying. He
finishes his cigarette and climbs, drowsy at last, into bed.
His thoughts mingle with dreams. He's climbing a ladder.
He's dancing. He's asleep.

"Ross, I've been thinking about Dodger. He wasn't up on that ladder as an act of charity. He was up there *hiding*." Martha's voice is robust, triumphant—the tone of political rallies. Ross opens his eyes. Though he seems to have been long asleep, the moon hasn't moved.

"What's that, Martha?"

"This Charles Bohannon lives on Main Street, right? On the highway?"

"Yes."

"So there you are. I've been lying here trying to figure it all out, and now I've got it." Martha lies on her back, her knees up. "Dodger comes to town pursued by the police, see. He's hitchhiked from God knows where, and he's passing through Willowby with a stranger who doesn't know he's a fugitive. Dodger realizes that the police are gaining on him, so when he sees this man painting this house, he asks the stranger to let him out of the car and he puts on the painters' coveralls and climbs the ladder. It's the perfect observation post. As he paints, he watches the traffic, and within fifteen minutes he sees what he's been looking for—obviously a police car passing down the street. And when the police are out of sight, he comes down off the ladder and heads out of town the opposite direction. Now isn't that more believable than your version, Ross? Your version is so sentimental. In my version Dodger isn't softhearted and Bohannon isn't his long-lost friend. The way I see it, Dodger is desperate and Bohannon is an unsuspecting accomplice."

Groggily, Ross gathers a few of his wits. "But, Martha, he made a point of coming here, to Willowby."

"Sheer coincidence. Willowby just happened to be

on his escape route. You're crediting Dodger with a sensitivity he couldn't possibly possess, given his background. You're trying to make a bleeding heart out of a hoodlum."

"Actually, I was trying to sleep."

"Sorry." Martha adjusts her pillow and blanket, bouncing the bed as she does so. "Good night, Ross." She's asleep in a minute, pleased with her logic.

Ross is wide-eyed. Sometimes, as now, he's tempted to envy Martha for her neatness of thought. How reassuring to see Dodger as Martha sees him, a hardened criminal, a crude, insensitive robber. How much easier on the conscience to think of Dodger—boy and man—as an unsalvageable wreck. How conducive to sleep.

And how impossible—for Ross's mind is now circling back to another memory, another vision perfectly preserved, poignantly clear. Ross's last sight of Dodger. It's the spring of 1944, April or May. Dodger has been absent from school for several days; he and his mother, it is said, are preparing to leave town. It's been a good year for Ross; he is a friend of everyone who counts, having distinguished himself at basketball, spelling, tree-climbing, kite-flying, and arithmetic. Today he is pumping himself high on a schoolyard swing; the Crowninshield twins, like court attendants, are swinging at his left hand and right. Suddenly Dodger appears, slouching toward school two hours late. Ross, still mildly ashamed of his treachery of last September, is dismayed to see him. He will be glad when Dodger is gone for good. Dodger heads straight for the swings, carrying a big new bag of marbles from the Five and Dime—a netlike bag, loosely woven out of stiff red string. He steps into the path of Ross's swing, forcing

Ross to skid to a stop. He tells Ross to stand up and hold his pocket open. Ross, smirking back at the twins, does as he is told. Dodger opens the bag and pours out marbles until Ross's pocket overflows. Until now, Ross has been playing marbles with a meager capital of about ten glassies and a couple of steelies—losing half a dozen a day, winning them back the next—and now all at once he has this wealth of glassies: three, four, five dozen spherical gems of swirling design, no two alike, the colors brilliant—amber, violet, crimson, brown. What do they mean? Are they life-signs in a friendship Ross assumed was dead? Are they Ross's reward for having eased Dodger's loneliness for two days last fall? Dodger doesn't explain. He merely nods when Ross says "Thanks," and he walks away, his stride long-legged and lazy, his wrists dangling from sleeves too short, the back of his head carelessly barbered. He leaves the schoolyard and crosses the street and disappears around a corner—never (hopes Ross, swinging with the twins) to return.

Agatha McGee

and the

St. Isidore Seven

WHEN THE PRINCIPAL of St. Isidore's Elementary, Sister Rose, announced that a faculty meeting would be held on Saturday morning in Axel's Tavern, the thoughtful and orderly Miss McGee had three thoughts, in this order: one, she thought that for a parochial school to hold its deliberations in a saloon was scandalous and surely the last stage in the Decline of the West; two, she thought she would not attend; and, three, she thought Sister Rose was out of her mind.

"Are you out of your mind?" she asked at lunch on Friday. "Why not call a meeting here and now? We're all present."

Miss McGee and Sister Rose were sitting at the faculty lunch table with the other five members of the staff. On Miss McGee's left, old Sister Raphael (first grade) and the gray-bearded Mr. Chambers (grades seven and eight combined) were discussing their fish sticks. Sister Raphael, who wore the black yard goods and white wimple of nuns of the old order, insisted that although the rules had changed, the voluntary avoidance of meat on Friday was still a virtue. Mr. Chambers wanted to know what was voluntary about eating fish sticks, which he detested, when the kitchen offered nothing else.

Across the table Sister Judy (fourth grade) and Mrs. O'Fallon (fifth) listened to Mrs. Mueller's account of a Jane Fonda movie she had seen, rated R. When Mrs. Mueller (grades two and three combined) got to the bedroom scene, Mrs. O'Fallon said, "Horrors." Sister Judy said, "Heavy."

"Tomorrow's meeting will be no ordinary faculty meeting," said Sister Rose from the head of the table. At this, the group fell silent. "We will be meeting with the teachers from the public school. It is they who have selected the place and time, and they have asked us to join them." Besides serving as principal, Sister Rose taught half-day kindergarten, belonged to the Governor's Commission on Women's Rights, and gave guitar lessons. Like Sister Judy, she was under thirty and had modified her habit to the point where the only remaining sign of her nunhood was a small silver cross pinned to the collar of her blouse.

"Why on earth would the public school teachers wish to meet with us?" said Miss McGee. This had been the first week of Miss McGee's forty-third year of teaching at St. Isidore's. An exhausting week. She had spent Labor Day laboring over lesson plans, Tuesday learning names and assigning desks and distributing textbooks, and Wednesday and Thursday giving diagnostic tests. Only this morning had she begun to feel that her sixth graders were adjusting to the goals and routines she had pre-scribed; finally she had them in harness for the long haul.

"I'm not at liberty to say any more," said Sister Rose. "We've been asked to help the public school staff carry out an extraordinary project, which will be explained to us tomorrow morning at ten."

"But in a saloon? Surely we could meet in the high school auditorium."

"It's the nature of the project that it must not be discussed on school property. They say the dance floor at the back of Axel's Tavern makes an ideal meeting room."

Miss McGee looked around the table. "Do any of you know what this is all about?"

"I have no idea," said Mrs. O'Fallon grumpily, "and furthermore a Saturday meeting strikes me as an imposition on our personal lives." Mrs. O'Fallon's interest in teaching was derived from her desire to earn the price of a new set of living-room furniture. Her husband was a farmer whose income went mostly into improving his herd of Guernseys.

"I know, but I'm not at liberty to say," said Mrs. Mueller, whose husband was the public school band director.

"I know too," said Sister Judy, "but all I can say is that it's something really heavy."

"Believe me, it's dynamite," said Mr. Chambers, who played poker once a week with a group of high school teachers.

"Surely you can tell your colleagues," said Miss McGee.

"Mum's the word," said Mr. Chambers, "but believe me, it'll knock your socks off." He dropped his napkin onto his plate, pushed his chair away from the table, and set to work combing breadcrumbs out of his beard.

"And you?" Miss McGee nudged the old nun on her left.

"Beg pardon?" Sister Raphael, savoring her fish sticks, had not been listening.

THE NEXT MORNING at ten all fifty-three teachers in town, public and parochial, were gathered in Axel's back room. This group included Miss McGee, who, never having had her socks knocked off, was too curious to stay home. She wore her navy blue suit and her white gloves and she moved through the crowd introducing herself to the few members of the public school staff she hadn't met—newcomers to town.

"Hello, I'm Agatha McGee, and I just want to say welcome to Staggerford."

For some reason, the newcomers knew her ("So *you're* Agatha McGee!") and one of them added, "We're hoping that you, of all people, will see our side of it."

"Your side of *what*, pray tell?"

"The strike."

"The meeting will come to order," someone shouted, and the crowd sat down on folding chairs. On the bandstand stood a set of drums, a bass fiddle, and Herbert Greeley, president of the Public School Faculty Association. Herbert Greeley had been a sixth-grade student of Miss McGee's in 1944. He wore thick glasses; his hair and suit were gray, his expression careworn. Above his head a neon sign blinked "BLATZ."

"Welcome to this emergency meeting," he began.

"For you who haven't heard what's going on, let me bring you up to date. The public school board, at its meeting Thursday night, voted to rescind its agreement of last spring concerning teachers' salaries. Originally the board had promised us a five percent raise, but now, faced with what it calls 'unforeseen expenses,' the board says we'll be paid according to last year's salary schedule."

Here, somebody booed. Somebody else cried, "Rip-off!"

"We have tried without success to convince the board that their decision is unfair, unforgivable, and unethical, but the board refuses to reconsider. Our association, therefore, has voted 35 to 11 to go out on strike first thing Monday morning and to picket the two public school buildings, elementary and secondary, until the five percent is restored."

Here, somebody cheered. Somebody else said, "Let's order a round of beer." Miss McGee was afraid the latter voice belonged to Mr. Chambers. She had nothing against beer, but coarse behavior made her cringe.

Herbert Greeley continued, bowing slightly in Miss McGee's direction, "Now of course this broken promise has no direct bearing on you people from St. Isidore's, but we're hoping that you will sympathize with our cause . . ."

A just cause, thought Miss McGee, who abhorred broken promises, *but striking is for teamsters, not teachers.*

". . . and that you will take an active part in supporting us . . ."

I'll have a word with the board members. I know them all.

". . . by going out on strike yourselves—a sympathy strike."

Lord in Heaven!

"With all of education shut down in Staggerford, the strike is likely to have a greater impact and end sooner, particularly since one of the board members has a child attending St. Isidore's, and another, a grandchild." Herbert Greeley looked at his watch. "And now as the association turns its attention to picketing schedules and other details of the strike, I wonder if Sister Rose and her staff would adjourn to another room and vote on whether St. Isidore's will join us in our effort. We'd be forever grateful for your help."

The St. Isidore Seven went into the dimly-lit barroom and sat at a round table and voted. The bartender, with no customers at the bar, eavesdropped.

Mr. Chambers voted to strike. He said he couldn't let his buddies down.

Sister Raphael said that striking was ungodly, and having said it, she stood up, gathered her robes about her, and hurried out the front door and back to the convent, her black veil trailing in the breeze.

Sister Judy said, "I vote in favor of striking because it's high time the Church took a stand on social issues."

Sister Rose said, "I agree with that, and moreover a strike will help move St. Isidore's into the mainstream of the community. Striking will give us a fresher image, a higher profile."

Three to one for striking. Mr. Chambers ordered a pitcher of beer and six glasses.

Mrs. O'Fallon, her mind on a couch and chair of brushed velvet, asked what a strike would do to her income.

"You'd lose a day's pay for every day of the strike," said Sister Rose. "But the strike will surely be short, especially if we join it."

"No," said Mrs. O'Fallon, "public school teachers already make twice as much as we do. I vote no."

Mrs. Mueller said a strike was bound to cause hard feelings. Her husband had been one of the eleven dissenters in the public school. She wouldn't think of voting against his wishes.

Three to three. "And you, Agatha?" said Mr. Chambers, pouring her a glass of beer.

Miss McGee was stumped. She removed her white gloves and spread them across her lap and folded her hands on the edge of the table. "Striking is unprofessional," she said. "How can we condone it?"

"Exactly," said Mrs. O'Fallon.

"But on the other hand, the school board's action was dishonest. Those forty-six people signed their contracts and went to work in good faith, and now the board has gone back on its word. How can we condone that?"

"Exactly," said Mr. Chambers.

She looked at the ceiling. "But a strike would set back the progress we have made this week in our classes. It would divide the parish into warring halves. It would upset our pastor."

Sister Rose said, "A yes from you would do a lot, Agatha. You have a very high profile in this town."

Miss McGee took a sip of beer and closed her eyes. Her fellow teachers were silent, respecting her meditation. Even the bartender folded his arms and hung his head.

After a minute, Sister Rose asked, "Do you say yes or no, Agatha?"

Her eyes popped open. She stood up and put on her gloves. "I say wait till tomorrow for my decision. I'm off to see the board." She left.

"Damn," said Sister Judy.

Sister Rose went into the next room to announce that her staff was deadlocked.

"Well anyhow, drink up, ladies," said Mr. Chambers, raising his glass.

"Maybe she can avert the strike," said Mrs. O'Fallon.

"I wouldn't put it past her," said the bartender.

THE SCHOOL BOARD, having been notified of the strike, held a special meeting on Saturday night, and Miss McGee was present. Though there were two empty chairs in the board room, no one asked her to sit, which was just as well since she did her best thinking on her feet. The five men of the board sat at a long, polished table on which there were five black notebooks and two white telephones. She addressed herself to the president, a young man named Jerry Logan, who owned an ice cream drive-in at the edge of town.

"I'm here to ask if it's true that you have reneged on your agreement concerning teachers' pay."

Jerry Logan, behind a screen of cigar smoke, nodded. "We have been faced with some very large and unforeseen expenses," he said. "Perhaps you haven't heard that on New Year's Day the Staggerford High School band will be marching in the Rose Bowl Parade." The four other men nodded proudly. Jerry Logan beamed. "We received the invitation on Thursday."

"How lovely, but what has that to do with salaries?"

Jerry Logan consulted his notebook. "Transportation, lodging, meals—fourteen thousand dollars. New band uniforms—nine thousand dollars. That's over half of the money earmarked for teachers' salaries."

"And the other half?"

"We're having new sod laid on the high school football field, Miss McGee, and a sprinkling system installed."

"Hardly an unforeseen expense."

"Oh but it is. The summer, as you know, was unusually dry. It turned the gridiron to dust. Our boys can't be expected to play on a gridiron without grass."

"Nor can teachers be expected to work for a school board without scruples. Don't tell me that all of you are in agreement with this unprincipled line of reasoning."

The four followers averted their eyes. Bartholomew Druppers, a lifelong neighbor of Miss McGee's, studied his cufflinks. Stan Billings, the undertaker, looked grieved. No one spoke.

"I see. In that case you all ought to be turned out of office. It's a scandal when our elected officials need to be reminded of the difference between right and wrong. First, let me remind you . . ."

"Miss McGee, our time is precious, and I'm afraid we can spare you no more of it." Jerry Logan's smile intensified; his smoke screen grew denser. "We are meeting tonight for the purpose of phoning prospective substitute teachers to fill in for the strikers, so you'll please excuse us now while we get on with our calling."

"How could you possibly hope to find four dozen substitutes in a town this size?"

"Are you forgetting that this is an era of surplus teachers, Miss McGee? From the placement offices of several colleges we have learned of sixty unemployed teachers living in this part of Minnesota." He held up a sheet of paper containing names and addresses and phone numbers. "To say nothing of the housewives and retirees who might be willing to help us out. Like it or not, Miss McGee, in this day and age all educators are expendable."

The four followers found a similar sheet in their notebooks and they studied it intently, glad of an excuse to look busy.

Jerry Logan continued, "We have the bull by the horns, Miss McGee, and we won't be intimidated by a faculty of strikers. Let me remind you that our first duty, as employers, is to use the taxpayers' money to their best advantage. By marching in the Rose Bowl Parade, and thus by appearing on national TV, our band will put Staggerford on the map. We're having signs erected at both ends of town announcing 'Staggerford, Home of the Rose Bowl Marching Band.' There's no measuring the good that can come from a thing like that. It will enhance our business climate. It's a principle of free enterprise that civic pride improves the flow of cash. Now, Miss McGee, besides expecting your football team to play on a field of dust, would you also deny your fellow citizens the joy of seeing their band in Pasadena? The joy of reading those two billboards? The joy that goes with civic pride? I realize your interests are narrow, Miss McGee, given your age and all, but I can't believe you're so coldhearted as to deny your fellow citizens all that joy."

Miss McGee leaned forward over the table, her

brow an astonishing pink. The four men on her left and right drew slightly back in their chairs. "Forty-six of my fellow citizens are people you have cheated, Mr. Logan, and it's left them something less than joyous. And I was about to say a moment ago when you interrupted me that it is wrong and reprehensible of you to break faith with your employees. You speak of spending money wisely, but where is the wisdom in the capricious breaking of a promise? You speak of free enterprise, yet when you pin all your hopes and dreams on the flow of cash you strike me as neither very free nor very enterprising. Now either you will restore the five percent or the schools will close, St. Isidore's included."

"St. Isidore's?" said Stan Billings, whose son, a shy seven-year-old, Sister Raphael was teaching to read.

"St. Isidore's?" said Bartholomew Druppers, whose grandson, a mouthy twelve-year-old, Miss McGee was training to hold his tongue.

"How can we possibly restore the five percent?" said Jerry Logan. "Our tax levy is limited. You can't squeeze blood from a turnip, Miss McGee."

"That's no harder than squeezing sod from a teacher's wallet, Mr. Logan. You might know a lot about ice cream but you don't know the first thing about integrity. Now what you must do is instruct the band members to get busy with fund-raising activities so that they can provide their own money for food and lodging and transportation. You must forget about new uniforms—have the old ones dry-cleaned and mended—and you must tell your football team that you're sorry about their playing in dust, and build a sprinkler into next year's budget. There, gentlemen, you have my viewpoint, narrow as it is, given my age and all."

"I seriously doubt that the band can raise fourteen thousand dollars in three months' time." Jerry Logan spoke through his cigar, its fire glowing and dimming like a pulse.

"Then they stay home, having learned something about the limits of life's possibilities—or else the merchants of Staggerford cough up the difference. Now if you come to your senses and restore the five percent before you adjourn tonight, please call me at home. Otherwise, I'll have to cast my lot with the strikers. And I must add, in closing, that I've never cared for the soft ice cream that comes out of your machines, Mr. Logan. Thank you. Good night."

She spun around and hurried through the next room to the outside door. She pushed the door open before she realized that a heavy rain was falling. She stepped back and let the door swing shut. She sat on a bench, intending either to wait out the rain or, if it persisted, to catch a ride with Bartholomew Druppers when the meeting ended. The door to the board room was open. She heard the clearing of throats and the mumbling of the four followers. She heard Jerry Logan say, "How much longer is this town going to put up with that old biddy? Isn't it about time somebody took away her digitalis?"

She shot into the board room so fast that Jerry Logan flinched and choked on his smoke. He coughed through his cigar, which erupted in a shower of sparks. Through his watery eyes, bereft of his voice, he saw her dialing one of the phones.

"Herbert Greeley," she said, "this is Agatha calling

and I have two things to say. First, you can count on St. Isidore's to join you in your strike and, second, I have in my hand"—she put out her hand and Bartholomew Druppers graciously gave her his sheet of paper—"the names and phone numbers of sixty unemployed, retired, and otherwise unoccupied teachers that the board is about to offer your jobs to. If you would be so kind as to pick me up at the south door of the high school, I will give you this list. I think your telephone committee should contact these people at once and explain the circumstances. Surely most of them will honor your strike. . . . Yes, Herbert, the south door. Alert your telephone committee. And please bring me seven of your picket signs, so that I can take them to St. Isidore's on Monday morning."

When she hung up, Bartholomew Druppers said, "Mr. Chairman, I move that we open the matter of faculty salaries to further discussion. I am no longer comfortable with our decision of last Thursday."

"Nor am I," said Stan Billings. "I second the motion."

The meeting was soon over. When Herbert Greeley came for Miss McGee, the board members were already running through the rain to their cars.

"The phone committee is ready," he said, pulling away from the curb. "Have you brought the sixty names and numbers?"

"No need for that now, Herbert. I bring you instead your five percent."

His face brightened, his eyes bulged. "You're joking!"

"I am not joking, Herbert. The board has voted four to nothing to reverse its reversal of Thursday night, but don't ask me to explain. In return for your five percent, they requested that I not divulge the details of the meeting. Some things were said that don't bear repeating, and besides that, I think the majority of members are ashamed of the awkward way they've handled things. They'd like it soon forgotten. Let's just say that they've been suddenly inspired with alternatives."

"But tell me, Agatha—four to nothing means someone abstained."

"Mr. Logan, the emperor of ice cream, abstained. When does his term expire, Herbert?"

"Next spring. But I can't imagine his not voting. He's the most outspoken member."

"Except for when he's on fire. At the time the vote was taken he seemed more interested in putting out the small fires that were smoldering in his shirt front and lap. Please don't ask me to explain."

AT LUNCH on Monday, Mrs. Mueller said that her husband and his band were busy organizing a car wash, a fish fry, and a bingo party.

Sister Raphael, separating her pork from her beans, told Mr. Chambers that meatlessness was a virtue any day of the week, not only on Friday.

"In that case," said Mr. Chambers distastefully, "this is the most virtuous helping of beans I've ever eaten."

Mrs. O'Fallon said she thanked her lucky stars that the strike had been averted and she had lost no pay.

Sister Judy said, "Aren't you sorry, Miss McGee, that you didn't cast your vote at Axel's Tavern? Here was a heavy moral issue, and you missed your chance to take a stand."

Miss McGee chuckled mysteriously. "Yes, I should have taken a stand. But come spring I intend to change my ways. I hereby declare my candidacy for the school board seat now occupied by Mr. Logan, whose term expires in May. Can I count on your support?"

"Praise the Lord," said Sister Rose. "A woman is exactly what that board has needed all along. Let us know when you're ready to kick off your campaign, Agatha. We'll hold a rally for you in Axel's Tavern."

"Amen," said Sister Judy.

"That's two votes. What about the rest of you."

"You have mine," said Mrs. O'Fallon, "and think of your hundreds of former students who will vote for you."

"You have mine," said Mr. Chambers, "and think of all the public school teachers who are fed up with Jerry Logan."

"And all their spouses as well," said Mrs. Mueller.

Miss McGee nudged the old nun on her left. "And you, Sister? How will you vote?"

"Striking is ungodly," said Sister Raphael, searching deep in her beans for an elusive shred of pork fat, "I vote no."

NANCY CLANCY'S
NEPHEW

WATER SPARKLED so bright in the street that George Post, sitting by the window, couldn't keep his mind on the morning paper. Snowbanks diminished before his eyes, uncovering patches of brown grass, and the old red oak in the front yard, having hung on to its leaves through fierce winter winds, released them now to a puff of warm air from the south.

"I'm going to see Nancy Clancy," he called from his chair.

This winter had been the worst of the seventy-five George Post could remember. Day after day the north wind had sucked a small, stinging snow out of a sky so hopelessly gray that the neighborhood cats, even the pretty ones, put on shaggy, dull coats and the family dog was content to lie for hours on rugs, moving only his eyes and the end of his tail. It seemed to George Post that the only break in the overcast had been the bitter stretch in January when the air itself froze and he couldn't see across the street through the icy haze until the sun burned through at noon and raised the temperature to 25-below. For sixty days he had been confined to the house. He had lost his patience early, and then he lost his impatience, reconciling himself to a daily schedule reduced to three activities: he smoked his pipe; he ate the meals his daughter, Mrs. Mullen, prepared for him; he read the morning paper, forgetting each paragraph as he went on to the next. His days became so simple and shadowless that he couldn't remember one from another, and it wasn't until this morning's sudden thaw that he remembered Nancy Clancy. Old plans, set aside as impossible in December, were worth considering again.

"I'm going to see Nancy Clancy," he said, his voice rumbling with phlegm.

Into the living room came his daughter, wiping her hands on her apron. She was sixty and married to a salesman named Mullen, who was seldom home. "What now?" she said.

"I'm going to see Nancy Clancy."

"What possessed you to think of Nancy Clancy?" Mrs. Mullen's hair, dyed so black it looked blue, was up in curlers.

"We used to visit her every so often."

"Who did?"

"My brothers and I. My cousins. You did yourself when you were a youngster."

Mrs. Mullen started back to the kitchen.

"Mind you, I'm going to see her," said George Post.

"All right. We'll plan a day."

"This afternoon," he said. "I'm going after lunch."
When he saw her turn to look at him, he took his pipe from
the pocket of his vest and examined the crusty bowl.

"I'm shopping this afternoon," she said. "I haven't
time for visiting."

"I'll take the bus."

"Don't be silly."

"I'll take the bus."

"The bus stops four blocks from here and six blocks
from Nancy's apartment. You're not up to it. You haven't
been out all winter." She spoke as though he were hard of
hearing.

George Post blew into the stem of his pipe until spit
bubbled in the bowl.

"Oh, all right," said Mrs. Mullen. "I'll drop you at her
apartment and pick you up on my way home. But make up
your mind to be there a while. I'm after a spring coat and
can't be hurried. And I'm meeting Florence Becker. She's
looking for a coat too."

After lunch it took Mrs. Mullen fifteen minutes to
transfer her father from his chair to the car. When they got
as far as the front hall, Mrs. Mullen said, "You don't need
your overcoat. It's a spring day."

"Tut," said George Post. He buttoned his vest and
put on his suitcoat and carefully crossed his white scarf
over his throat and struggled into his black overcoat while
Mrs. Mullen stood holding his gloves, his hat, and his cane.
She thought, without fondness, of the winters when her
children were small and of the trouble it was to dress them
to go out.

Without help, George Post shuffled through a puddle of melting ice on the front sidewalk, moving each foot
an inch at a time and leaning heavily on his rubber-tipped
cane. Halfway through the puddle he stopped to survey
the distance he had come and, turning, he nearly lost his
balance. Mrs. Mullen offered her hand but he pulled his
elbow away and resumed his shuffle.

Never before had he found it necessary to bend himself to fit a bucket seat. As Mrs. Mullen held the door open
for him, he stood at the curb studying the seat. It was too
low. If he hadn't come so far, he would have turned back.
Finally, closing his eyes, he fell into the car and dragged
his cane and his legs in after him. Mrs. Mullen slammed
the door and hurried around to the driver's side. The car
was small and orange and it tilted when she got in.

"See if you can find out her age, at least," she said,
tidying her hair in the mirror. "For all the trouble we're
going to, you ought to come out of it with something." She
started the car with a roar and set out across the city.

George Post was the last family survivor of his generation and Nancy Clancy was his aunt. Her age was a mystery, but she was thought to be near one hundred. From her
apartment, into which she had been crammed with a surplus of household goods after her last brother died, she kept
track, by letter, of a dozen branches of the family and she
emerged for holiday dinners, at which she was not loved but
admired like an heirloom and always delivered home earlier
than she wished to be. It was to Nancy Clancy that births,
weddings and deaths were first announced.

Mrs. Mullen drove with a heavy foot. Downtown she
nearly collided with a bus and on a residential street she

would have hit a man on a bicycle if he hadn't steered himself into a driveway where he tipped over in a pool of slush. Both times she glanced at her father and assured herself that he hadn't noticed. He noticed, but he said nothing.

"What possessed you to think of Nancy Clancy?" she said. "You've never been one to pay calls."

"It's March," said George Post.

She parked in front of a stone apartment building and said, "Find out if she's a hundred." She reached across her father and opened his door, then she steadied him as he got to his feet. When he stood free of the car she said, "I'll be back at five and you be down. I don't want to climb those godawful stairs. Don't leave your gloves or your hat up there." Racing the engine as she shifted gears, she shot away from the curb so that the open door closed itself.

Teetering at the curb, George Post found himself between a snowbank and a small boy who, like himself, was bundled up for winter.

"Was that your mother?" asked the boy.

"No," said George Post. As a rule he ignored children, but this one struck his fancy because he spoke so clearly for his size. He stood no higher than George Post's cane.

The boy walked at his side to the entrance of the building and asked, "Do you live here?"

"No."

"Who lives here?"

"Nancy Clancy."

"Who's that?"

George Post stopped and pointed his cane at a third-floor window. "She lives up there and she's a hundred."

"A hundred years *old*?"

George Post climbed the two steps to the heavy front door and pushed it open.

"Some turtles are a hundred," the boy said as he watched the heavy door swing shut.

There was no elevator in the building and George Post paused with both feet on each step, like a pilgrim approaching a shrine. Halfway up the second flight he felt giddy. A fountain seemed to be rising up his spine and bubbling in his brain, a sensation like the one he was allowed on Christmas afternoons when red wine was in good supply. He hooked his cane over his arm and gripped the banister with both hands. The fountain gradually subsided, but it sprang to life again when he took the next step. Several minutes passed before he reached the top step, where he leaned against the wall, tense and queasy. He felt as though he had outdistanced some vital part of himself—his lungs, his soul—and he was waiting for it to catch up. His right foot was asleep and he poked it with his cane.

In the dark hall a scrap of paper was taped to the first door he came to, and on it was shakily printed *Miss N. Clancy.* Through the door came the sound of a piano, a jangling combination of treble keys which he interrupted with a loud rap.

"Who is it?" called a thin voice.

"George." He took off his hat.

"Who?"

"George Post. Your nephew George."

The door opened and there stood Nancy, short and wrinkled and skinny as a stick, with her cheek out to be kissed. Her thick glasses were ice blue.

"Glory be," she said as he pecked her cheek. A faded

blue dress hung down to her high black shoes and a flimsy dustcap hung over one ear. The weightless hand she offered him felt like five cold twigs.

He was about to tell her she was looking younger all the time, but she seemed alert enough to know better. "You look just the same," he said.

"Of course I do. You reach a point when it's impossible to look any older. Sit down. I was scrubbing my piano keys." She snatched a rag and a can of Bon Ami off the piano stool and disappeared into her kitchen. She was quicker than George Post remembered her.

He slowly removed his gloves and overcoat and lowered himself into a velvet chair by the piano. He set a crystal ashtray on his lap and rapped it with his pipe. The ashtray broke in half. He studied the ranks of fading photographs on the piano, the men choked into high stiff collars and the ladies in plumed hats. Each face wore a serious expression and the men looked as substantial as bankers, even the young ones, but they were fading all the same.

"The surprise of my life, seeing you, George," said Nancy, returning with a letter in her hand and settling lightly on the center cushion of her davenport. It dipped only slightly, like a bough under a bird. She had removed her dustcap and George Post saw that her hair, like her piano keys, had gone from white to yellow.

"I'm here till five," he said. "Margaret's coming by at five." He reached to a coffee table and exchanged the two halves of the crystal ashtray for a brass bowl.

"It's been thirty years since you paid me a call."

"Fiddlesticks. I helped you move into this apartment."

"That's not paying a call, George. I mean a proper call."

"Well, here I am. Till five." He beat the bowl with his pipe.

When the ringing died away Nancy said, "Did you hear Gertrude passed on?" He nodded. "Trudy she called herself after she moved to Oregon. Now all my nieces and nephews are dead, George, except you."

He had serious blockage in his pipe, and he was turning red trying to blow through the stem. "You never had much to do with Gertrude, anyway," he said finally. "None of us did."

"Makes no difference. At least she was *there*. Here is her last letter to me." Nancy slipped a page out of the envelope and offered it to him but he waved it away.

"She's buried in the West," he said.

"Glory be, is that any reason for not reading her last words? Did you leave your glasses at home?"

"What glasses? I don't wear glasses any more." He was still busy with his pipe. "My sight is improving with age. Coming over here with Margaret, I read the numbers on moving boxcars. I haven't worn glasses for ten years."

"Well, it's nothing to get uppity about," said Nancy. "The eyesight in our family has never been remarkable."

"Except mine. Mine is remarkable." He set his plugged pipe on the coffee table. "It was your brother Len that had the worst eyesight I ever saw short of a blind man. He tied a white handkerchief to the steering wheel of his E M F. Now don't deny it."

"My stars, why should I deny it? That was the way he drove to town and back, with the handkerchief tied to the top of the steering wheel. That way he could tell if he was steering straight ahead. The road wasn't plain to him, but the handkerchief was."

"One day I was driving my Overland out north of Pinburg," said George Post, pointing into the kitchen as though Pinburg were behind the refrigerator, "and I looked around and there was Uncle Len in his E M F coming up behind me faster than blazes. He was trying to catch up to me and he was laying a dust cloud over the land." He began to chuckle. "That was his way. Catch up behind somebody he could see and follow him into town. You know how the road makes a jog around that big rock pile north of Pinburg. Well, I turned left to follow the road and Len lost sight of me and thought the rock pile was the back end of my Overland. He drove straight into the rock pile."

His laugh was silent, but it grew until it shook him like a convulsion. He rolled his head helplessly and bared his bad teeth. Then he squirmed around in his chair and pulled a handkerchief out of his back pocket to mop his tears.

"Wasn't it the Model-A he drove into the rock pile?" said Nancy. "Or was it the Studebaker?"

"It was the E M F," said George Post, recovering. "Every Morning Fix'em."

"It's a wonder he wasn't killed that time."

"The ditch slowed him down. It was a sandy ditch."

"But it was the E M F he died in."

"Yes, it was the E M F he died in." George Post shook again with mirth. "He took Harold McGivern's best team with him, too. He was east of Pinburg that time. Nobody knew what he was doing east of Pinburg. His place was north. He caught sight of Harold McGivern's team and wagon and he raced down the road like blazes to catch up with it. Only trouble was . . ." he laughed silently, then said from behind his handkerchief, "Only trouble was Harold McGivern was coming instead of going."

Nancy folded her arms, not amused.

With a sudden sober expression George Post struggled out of his chair, the brass bowl falling from his lap.

"Where's the bathroom?"

"Through the kitchen," said Nancy, pointing.

"Harold McGivern jumped clear, but Uncle Len and the team hit head-on and tangled up and died," said George Post, shuffling into the kitchen with wet pants.

"The door by the range," Nancy called after him.

The phone rang, and on her way to answer it Nancy replaced the brass bowl on the table and smoothed the doilies on the arms of the velvet chair.

It was Mrs. Mullen calling.

"I dropped Dad off at your place. Did he get upstairs all right?"

"Yes, he's here. My, he's failed."

"I just wanted to say I'll stop back at five."

"Five will be just fine. We were just talking about Leonard."

"Who?"

"My brother Leonard. It will be forty years ago August that he died in the accident."

"I won't have time to run up to the apartment, Nancy. I would like you to send him down at five."

"And you know, Margaret, it will be fourteen years next week that Wilfred, the last of my brothers, died and I said to myself, 'Nancy, you're next. The Lord has taken the boys first and one of these days He'll be tapping you on the shoulder.' But He never did. The next thing I knew He was picking and choosing among the next generation younger than me. In fourteen years now I've seen eight nieces and nephews called, one by one, and I've been there in my black hat to see most of them blessed and buried."

"Five o'clock then."

"And from the looks of George Post I expect to be in the mourners' pew at least once more. I knew the minute I opened the door and looked him in the eye. I could tell by his color."

"He had a spell in January, but he's better now."

"He's the color of chalk. And he's losing control of his bodily functions."

"Five o'clock then. Don't let him forget his hat and gloves."

"He's my last nephew, Margaret. George Post is all that's left between my generation and yours. He's my last bridge."

"And his scarf. And take care of yourself, Nancy."

"It's not myself I'm . . ."

"Goodbye then."

"And his sense of humor isn't what it was," Nancy said to the dial tone.

She hung up and took the broken crystal ashtray to the kitchen. She dropped it into a garbage sack and reached to a high shelf for two flowered teacups.

George Post and Nancy had tea in the kitchen and disagreed about the date when Nancy had moved into the apartment.

"It was the fall of fifty," said George Post, "because

we called on three darkies to move the piano and I gave them each a dollar."

"The fall of fifty I was in Chicago visiting Viola."

"It had to be the fall of fifty because you said, 'Pay the darkies and I'll pay you back' and I gave them each a dollar and you never paid me back. I've been out three dollars since the fall of fifty." He scooped three spoons of sugar into his tea.

"We called on one colored to help with the piano, not three." Trying to speak forcefully, Nancy's voice cracked. "Back then there weren't three colored in the entire city. And you gave him three dollars and I paid you back later in the day."

They fell silent. Nancy reached into a covered dish and drew out a prune. George Post looked out the kitchen window. A sharp breeze rippled the puddles in the alley, but they did not sparkle. Clouds had moved over the city and it looked wintry again.

After tea, Nancy brought her photograph album to the kitchen and served it to George Post like a plate of food. She carefully opened the velvet cover and pulled her chair closer as he squinted at a picture in which his father was a boy and Nancy was a baby. They were among a group of picnickers in bonnets and suspenders.

"That was out in Uncle Len's pasture by the creek," said George Post. "I remember it was the day Doc Anderson went by in his buggy and it wasn't till later we heard Hilda Vanderveer had triplets. There's me and my sister. Just youngsters."

"That's not you. That's your father," said Nancy. "And that baby girl is me. It shows the family twenty years before you were born." Nancy smoothed down the tattered black page. "It's the first picture in our family ever. And I'm in it."

"That's me as a youngster, Nancy," George Post insisted, uncurling his little finger and pressing it on the boy in the photograph. "And my sister is by my side."

"Can't you understand? That baby girl is me and I'm older than you. I'm older than you, George, by more than a little." Nancy spit a prune pit into her hand.

"If it wasn't the day of Hilda Vanderveer's triplets, what was Doc Anderson doing going by?"

"George, this wasn't the day Doctor Anderson went by. You're thinking of another day. This was before Doctor Anderson ever set up practice in Pinburg."

"Who's this, then?" asked George Post, quickly turning the page. "It looks like Uncle Sherman in his overalls."

Nancy moved in for a closer look. "That's who it is."

"See? What did I tell you? And his dog."

"Yes, his dog. His farmhouse stands to this day on the edge of Pinburg—what's left of Pinburg."

On the next page they studied a photograph of George Post in a baptismal dress. Further on they saw Leonard with one foot on the running board of his E M F. They spent the rest of the afternoon absorbed in the album, speaking low, like sleepers mumbling in a dream.

At twenty to five Mrs. Mullen called to say she was starting out.

"He'll be at the curb," said Nancy. "He just now started down the stairs."

"Did you have a nice visit?"

"Yes. He talks of coming again, now that he's broken the ice."

"That would be nice. I'm giving Florence Becker a ride home so you understand why I can't run up."

"Margaret, have you ever known him to be dizzy?"

"Dizzy? In January he had dizzy spells."

"What did the doctor say?"

"We didn't have him see the doctor. He got over them by himself."

"Really, Margaret, I think he should be looked at good and proper. The doctor straightened out Wilfred once when he was unsteady like that. There's a medicine for it."

"We'll see how he comes along. Take care of yourself, Nancy."

"He's my bridge."

Mrs. Mullen was calling from a pay phone in a parking lot. She hung up and turned to Mrs. Becker.

"Now he's talking about going back for another visit. It reminds me of the children when they had to be carted clear across the city to scouts and birthday parties."

"I don't know how you do it, Margaret. You must be one of God's own saints the way you've taken care of him all these years. And it isn't only me that says so. The girls at bridge say it." The preparation on Mrs. Becker's face was drying and lightly sprinkling the collar of her new coat.

An attendant delivered the orange car. They got in and found themselves in rush-hour traffic. As Mrs. Mullen inched her way out of the parking lot through a crowd of pedestrians, a flurry of snow dusted the windshield. There was a cold, pink light in the sky but at street level, between the tall buildings, it was dusk.

Once in the street, Mrs. Mullen waited several minutes for a line of cars to move. She looked in the mirror and patted her hair. "Did I ever tell you, Florence, how old we think Nancy Clancy is? We think she's a hundred."

"A hundred years *old?*" Think of it."

"We'll find out for sure when we pick up Dad. I told him to find out. But, Florence, I'm afraid when we pick him up you'll have to ride in back. It's all he can do to get in and out of the front seat and if we once got him in the back seat I'm afraid we'd never get him out, his joints are so stiff. Would you mind terribly?"

"Nonsense. It's little enough to do. But if Nancy Clancy lives on Laurel, I really could walk from there. It can't be more than six blocks."

"No, no, no. You're alone for supper and I'm alone for supper. We're going to take Dad home. I'll fix him his soup, then you and I will go out to eat."

"Well . . ."

"And maybe take in a movie."

"I should really fix my face."

"Fix it at my house."

Mrs. Mullen found clear sailing down a one-way street and stepped on the gas. Snowflakes, like shooting sparks, flashed in the headlights.

THE LITTLE BOY who spoke so clearly for his size lay on a wet snowbank with his mouth open, waiting for a snowflake to fall in. He was looking up at a streetlight around which falling snow hovered like a swarm of moths. Then he heard a bell and sat up. The ringing was new to the neighborhood and after a minute he got to his feet and followed the sound across several front yards. The snowbanks he stepped in were crusty, and the grass was freezing crisp and slippery under the light, new snow. He stopped in front of the stone apartment house and looked up to the third floor. It was not a bell; it was an old lady extending her thin wrists out through the narrow space under the hinged storm window. She was banging a brass bowl with a pipe. She dropped the bowl when she saw the boy and she put her face down to the opening.

"There he is and what did I just tell Margaret?"

To understand her, the boy had to stand directly beneath the window.

"There he is behind you," she said, and the boy turned to see a dark shape on the snow. He approached it and recognized the old man who had told him of the hundred-year-old lady. He saw his cane upright in a snowbank and his hat on a sheet of thin ice that had earlier been a puddle. The old man was scowling. The boy snatched at his sleeve and raised an arm, but the old man did not help himself up. He scowled. He seemed determined to stay where he was. Looking back at the old lady's window, the boy saw she still had her face to the opening and he returned to stand against the wall where he could hear her better.

"I came to the window to tell him he forgot his pipe," she was saying at the top of her small voice, "and I saw him fall. He's dead. The way he fell I know he's dead. He collapsed. Didn't I say I'd see the poor man dead? I no more than said it and he died. And he wasn't anywhere near born when that picture was taken in Leonard's pasture by the creek. I've called Father Melvin and I've called Doctor Fergusson, but he's dead. I can tell you that." She was stuffing something through the opening under the window. "Here's my afghan to cover him. He should be covered until help comes."

The afghan, worn thin as tulle, fluttered to the ground. The boy picked up a corner of it and took a few steps toward the dead man, but when he saw a car stop at the curb and the woman on the near side shrink back from the window and the other woman get out and come around past the headlights to the sidewalk saying "What now?" he dropped the afghan and ran home.

Agatha McGee · River Street · Staggerford, Minnesota

Dear Ones,

If you've met an elderly lady with a white-haired
gentleman who pushes a black, four-wheeled walker along
Minnehaha Parkway, you've seen me and my friend the
novelist out for a walk. (I have reluctantly agreed to
spend time at his home in Minneapolis because he is
amusing himself these days by making me the subject of
yet another novel.)

You may not have noticed his dreadful companion,
Dr. Parkinson, because he's quite evasive when we're
out in public, but he's never far away. Dr. Parkinson,
having lived with my friend for the past six years,
has begun to behave in cruel and irritating ways. He
has rendered the novelist's handwriting illegible, has
caused him to fall down a number of times (the cur-
rent number being 93), and has lowered his voice to
the point where it's hard to understand.

"He's quite a practical joker," my friend, out
walking, says of the despicable doctor. "I've been
giving quite a few public readings this season, in
connection with two new books I've written,* and I
find myself at a disadvantage, because I'm gradually
losing my ability to perform the three tasks necessary
for a reading; namely, walking up to the podium, reading aloud, and autographing."

The novelist has so far adjusted to these three
disabilities by demanding a good microphone, by ini-
tialing instead of autographing his books, and by
using his new, state-of-the-art walker, which features
hand brakes like a bicycle, a basket for carrying
things, and a seat for resting on.

But ninety-three is an alarming number of times
to fall down, and I ask him to explain how it happens.

*KEEPSAKES & Other Stories (Afton Historical Society Press, Afton Minnesota) and
My Staggerford Journal (Ballantine Books, New York).

"I freeze starting out," he tells me. "Once I'm on my way I'm fine; it's the first two or three steps that cause me to stumble."

"And how are you able to avoid serious injury?"

"Mostly I fall on the carpet at home," he says in his typically Pollyanna style. It gets my goat the way he's always looking for the silver lining in the darkest of clouds. So I press him:

"But surely you can't fall on the carpet every time."

"No, you're right. Sometimes I fall on the tile floor in the kitchen and now and then on the sidewalk. I don't recommend either one—they're painfully hard, and I have bruises to show for them but so far no broken knees or hips. My bones are proving indestructible."

"You'd better not press your luck, my friend."

"Don't worry, Agatha, I'm experimenting with ways to avoid the total freeze-up. One method I've discovered is pausing before I step out. If I wait long enough, I can usually convince my feet to go where I want them to. Of course, this method can be embarrassing, especially if I'm standing in a doorway and people are waiting to come through."

"So in that case you go to another method?"

"Actually no. So far the pausing method is the only one I've hit on."

"How long do you stand there?"

"Around ten seconds, it used to be five."

"So what goes through your head while you're pausing? Surely it's frustrating."

"I pray," he says.

My astonishment must show on my face, for he goes on to explain:

"I've never been very good at praying, you see, because I've always had too much on my mind. Then one day it occurred to me that since I had nothing else to fill those few seconds, I would think about God for a change. Thank him for the beautiful autumn we've had this year, for example. Ask him questions."

"What questions?"

"Well, my main one of course is, why have I been burdened with this aggravating disease."

"And what does he say?"

"Nothing. You know God, he's very slow to speak."

"You have to give him more than ten seconds."

"Oh, I will, Agatha. I'll be up to fifteen seconds by spring."

At this point I change the subject, for his talk is bordering on the blasphemous. I take him back to his public appearances. "Do you foresee the day when you will no longer give readings?" I ask him.

"Of course, and soon," he says, with eagerness in his voice. "Then I can stay home and get more writing done."

"But how are you able to write, with your atrocious penmanship?"

"Oh, I gave up longhand a very long time ago. I write on a computer nowadays."

"You're able to hit the right keys, are you?"

"Eventually I am. While it's true that I average ten or twelve mistakes per line, I'm a compulsive reviser, so that's no problem."

Then we pause for a stoplight, and when it turns green and I'm waiting for him to get started, that's when it dawns on me. God has answered his question. I hesitate to tell him for fear he'll respond with a joke, but I blurt it out anyhow, crossing the street: "God has caused you to freeze in order to get your attention."

This stops him again. He looks at me very intently, and says, "That's why I love you, Agatha. You have all the answers." He appears not to be joking.

"Not all," I tell him modestly. Though I do.

Yours truly,

Agatha

Jon Hassler, Regent's Professor Emeritus at St. John's University (Minnesota), lives with his wife Gretchen in Minneapolis, where he is at work on a another novel about Agatha McGee and her friends and neighbors.

Designed by
Mary Susan Oleson
Afton, Minnesota

Typefaces are
Palatino and
Poetica Chancery